ONE CHRISTMAS IN *Snowdonia*

KELLY MATTHEWS

One Christmas in Snowdonia
by
Kelly Matthews

Other books by Kelly Matthews:
The Gift of Christmas
Christmas Magic at the Tenby Crystal Shop
Christmas Eve at Piccadilly Circus

Chapter One

This is not the way I want to end another year. Holly sat at her desk full of unwanted Christmas cheer. A singing Santa Claus that swayed his big butt to *A White Christmas*, Elvis style and tacky red and green tinsel draped over her computer monitor that moulted onto the keyboard. For the last two years she had worked at *The World* newspaper offices in London as a junior writer, but lately she'd been suffering from a severe lack of job satisfaction since being given the agony aunt section. She cursed the day she mentioned her counselling course to her boss as all she wanted to do was write real, human-interest stories, not give advice to middle-aged men on dating.

She slumped over the desk, staring at her screen. She reckoned she'd read the same line at least a dozen times but felt too comfortable to move to do anything her boss considered "work". Lunch break wasn't for another hour and despite her best efforts, the article she was reading bored her senseless, even though she had spent most of the morning writing it. With her left hand resting under her chin, she figured she'd chill until she had to get up from her sumptuous leather seat.

It wasn't long before she began to drift off to sleep, when the ping of a notification snapped her back to the day job.

"URGENT"

'Now what do you want, Lewis?'

Sitting up, she covered her mouth to stifle a yawn and brought the cursor to click open.

"JINGLE BELLS, JINGLE BELLS, JINGLE ALL THE WAY," blasted from the speakers, making her jump so hard, she pushed her leather chair backwards and toppled over the side, falling onto the wooden floor. The office erupted into fits of laughter, but she failed to see the humour. Having worked at the newspaper for the last two years, she thought her colleagues would've outgrown their childish behaviour by now. It wasn't like she was the new girl anymore.

'Bloody hell; Holly, are you alright?' asked a concerned Emily, with an outstretched hand.

Emily had been Holly's friend since she began working at *The World*. They often referred to each other as the sister they never had.

Holly scoffed. 'Do I look it? And you can wipe the smirk from your lips too,' she huffed, accepting her help. *Jingle Bells* continued to play, and on the screen was a countdown calendar for Christmas.

Lewis, the office joker rushed around the labyrinth of desks to her aid, but stopped short when he saw she had her hands on her hips with a look that was potentially lethal.

'It was just a joke, Holly Green,' he guffawed, but step back slowly towards his desk with his hands held in the air.

'Look, isn't taking the piss out of my name wearing a bit thin with you? Every bloody Christmas you make the same jokes, Lewis. Are you that dumb you can't come up with something more original than a calendar to annoy me on the first of bloody December?'

Now everyone's eyes were on Lewis, and they laughed even harder at his expense.

Lewis's face flushed as red as Santa's rosy cheeks on the picture behind him.

'I pity anyone receiving a gift from you, you must be so boring,' she continued and bent down to pick up her chair. 'And yes, Holly Green, that's my name; don't wear it out.'

A welcomed round of applause broke out around the room. Holly mockingly bowed and sat back down at her desk, wondering if she'd ever get a promotion. Writing the daily agony aunt section was becoming tiresome. She needed something exciting in her life.

'Lunch break, Holly,' said Emily, poking her arm. 'Do you want to go to the coffee shop or canteen today?' she yawned, stretching out her arms.

'Is it lunch already? I'm surprised it flew by to be honest.'

'Still bored of writing the agony aunt page, huh?'

'You bet. Surely there's got to be more to life than reading about other people's problems for a paltry wage.'

'Well, why haven't you asked Vivien if she has something else for you?'

'I guess I could ask. I've been too comfortable for a while, you know, just grateful for a job, but now...'

'Come on,' said Emily getting up from her seat. 'Let's eat first. So what'll it be, café or canteen?'

Thinking about the morning's entertainment courtesy of Lewis she decided she'd go to the canteen. Besides, it was raining and the only way to get over the humiliation was to face it head on.

'I'm not going to show them he got the best of me.' She picked up her handbag from under her desk and stood up, hitching down her skirt as she did so. 'I'm not saying that he did, you know.'

'Oh I know,' Emily snorted with laughter. 'He's just the office joker, even if his jokes *are* so bad they shouldn't be considered jokes.'

They walked together down the corridor to the escalator to take them to the third floor. The door was about to close and Holly shouted for them to hold the door, but an annoying, smirking, Lewis mockingly waved at them just as the door slammed shut.

'Did I tell you how much that guy annoys me?'

They both looked at each other.

'Many times,' they replied in unison and then began laughing as the headed for the stairs.

AT THE CANTEEN, CHRISTMAS was in full swing. Holly joined the back of the long queue, and looked up at the chalkboard on the glass counter.

Gingerbread Flavoured Coffee Available Today

She scoffed. Christmas spirit was everywhere, and now left alone with her thoughts, here she was, another year at *The World* Newspaper still writing the agony aunt section and another year without her fiancé. What happened to all their dreams, to the plans they had made for their future? Her thoughts were becoming depressing, and she knew she needed to snap out of it.

Deciding to skip the festive coffee, she ordered a cappuccino and a cheese baguette and sat next to Emily.

'I didn't mean to laugh earlier,' she said in all seriousness while stabbing a fork into her cold salad.

'Forget about it. I wasn't angry at all. I just wanted to scare him off but I think it had the reverse effect.'

'You certainly scared the rest of us. Apparently, he's been talking to Jack, feeling guilty so don't be alarmed if he comes and apologises later. You'll never know, he may be that dull, he'll buy you a real calendar as a way to say sorry,' she laughed hysterically into her cup of coffee.

'And I'll know where I'll shove it.'

'It's not a bad name though, Holly Green. I can see how people associate it with Christmas though…'

'I don't see the joke myself, and anyway I don't know how I'm going to get through Christmas this year for reasons you know well,' she said, forcing herself not to cry at the memory.

'Come on, Holly. I know this time of year is difficult for you, but you've got to try to let go sometime. Dan wouldn't want to see you like this.' She spooned another sugar into her coffee and took a sip.

Dan was Holly's fiancé, a soldier who was killed during active duty. It had been a little over a year but the feelings were still raw. Holly decided to paint a smile on her face, blanking out her friend's words. It wasn't that she didn't agree with her sentiments, it was because she felt embarrassed to have put her friend on the spot again. Sympathy was the last thing she wanted.

'I used to get the piss taken out of me at school because of my name. I'm sure my parents decided to call me Holly because my birthday falls in December, imagine if it was Easter, would you like to be called, Bunny?' She laughed. 'But there you go… I've got to live with it.'

An excited commotion between the writers on the next table intrigued them enough to look over.

'What's going on?' asked Emily.

'Haven't you heard?' said Brody, the head writer walking past their table. 'The Christmas article is up for grabs. Felicity has gone into labour.'

Holly swallowed her hot chocolate too quickly, burning the back of her throat. Both girls looked at each other with shocked expressions. Emily's eyeballs were bulging.

'Can you believe it? Vivien has to pick another writer for the job. Imagine, Holly, writing the world's best loved article of the year. You'd be famous.'

Holly coughed and grabbed a bottle of water out of her bag.

'Me?'

'You've got to go for it, hell, beg her if you must.'

'What about you?'

Emily waved her hand. 'I'm happy doing what I do but you…this is your opportunity to move on from the agony pages. And boy are they agony, the pages literally scream in pissing agony,' she laughed, 'no offence intended.'

'They do, I must admit. It's so depressing writing them. Okay, so what do I do, should I go and ask her straight out?'

About to take another sip on her hot chocolate, she saw the canteen door swing open; surprised to see her boss, Vivien Walker heading towards her. She came to a standstill by a table occupied with staff writers.

'Could I have your attention a moment,' she shouted. The canteen hushed and all eyes were on her. 'I have some bad news and good news. Let's get the bad over with first. Felicity, the girl who was writing the Christmas feature had to take early maternity leave, so the good news is, I need someone else to write it as it requires a little paid holiday.'

There were gasps and shocked faces around the room. Emily began hitting Holly's hand so hard.

'Ask her,' she whispered.

Holly couldn't speak for excitement. The whole canteen came to a standstill, waiting with anticipation of who will write the famous Christmas feature.

'Holly, have you got a moment? I need a favour,' she began and came towards her table. 'I want to ask you a favour...'

Oh here goes, Holly thought, biting her tongue. She had a feeling Vivien was going to ask her to cover Annie's family announcement section. It wouldn't be the first time she favoured her for the worst writing jobs.

'Felicity has asked me if I'd consider giving the job to you. Now I know you've wanted to try your hand at something new, so I agreed with her. You're a fine writer, Miss Green, so let's see what you can do with this.'

Emily dropped her fork into her bowl; the noise breaking the shocked silence of the room.

'Way to go, Holly,' she fisted the air amid looks from everyone.

Stunned, Holly was unable to formulate a word. Emily kicked her leg from under the table and she came to her senses.

'I'd love the opportunity, Miss Walker, thank you, thank you so much,' she got up, shaking the woman's hand.

'Good, well it's a human-interest story, ten thousand's words by the 20th and it must have a Christmas element, obviously. I'm counting on you; don't let me or the paper down.'

Holly could barely contain her excitement. 'I will deliver it before the deadline...'

'Don't rush it, you still have...'

'Nineteen days,' she said, remembering the calendar that appeared on her PC that morning.

'Yes, so good luck...Oh one more thing. Anna already had a story in mind and was heading to some quaint village in Snowdonia. I have the details and hotel sorted for you but as for everything else, you'll have to contact her.'

'Did you say you want me to go to Snowdonia?'

'Yes, and before you head on home, call into my office so I can sort you out with addresses and petrol allowance.'

'No problem and thank you again for this opportunity.' Her head swooned with the shock and surprise, and she sat back down worrying if she was good enough.

At that moment, the entire canteen stood and clapped her victory; and many came to personally congratulate her, even Lewis who couldn't apologise enough.

When everyone settled back down to their lunch, Holly turned to Emily, smacking her hand over her forehead.

'You'll never guess what I forgot? In all the excitement, I forgot, today is my dad's retirement party, I haven't got him anything yet and mum has organised a get together for this evening.'

Emily looked at her mobile. 'You've still got twenty-five minutes left for lunch, why don't you pop out now?'

'I could do,' she got to her feet. 'Are you coming?'

'Nah, if you don't mind. I'll catch you later.'

Chapter Two

'All finished?' asked Emily, pulling on her coat. 'You know, that could be your last post for the agony aunt section.'

Holly exhaled, hit the send button and relaxed back into her seat.

'Yeah I've finally finished and I hope so. But now I have to get to mum's house for the party.' She looked up at the big windows overlooking London. The lights of the city twinkled against the night sky. 'Gosh, where has the day gone?'

'Spent knee deep in other people's problems,' she winked. 'Anyway, I'm officially on holiday now, so I'll see you when you get back from your trip, you jammy bugger,' she waved.

'Yeah, see you, Em. I'll speak to you later. No doubt I'll need an excuse to escape the family at some point.'

As she walked out of the office doors, Emily turned back. 'Oh, and congratulations again, you deserve it.'

'Thanks, and I appreciate your support today. A bottle of Prosecco is winging its way to you as I speak.'

Emily gave her the thumbs up and then closed the office door behind her.

The computer monitor shut down. The office was now empty, and Holly got up from her seat, put on her coat and headed downstairs.

She stood in the foyer, facing the glass sliding doors and buttoned up her coat. Outside, the fierce wind blew the rain up the street. London was busy tonight. Despite the terrible storm, the traffic still whizzed by as normal, and people passed with their umbrellas blown inside out. Holly's heart sank. She wasn't thrilled about driving tonight, but there was no way she could miss her dad's party.

'If you're waiting for it to stop, you'll be there all night,' said a voice approaching her.

'Hi, Charlie,' she said to the door man. 'I think you're right, it's in for the night, isn't it?'

'I can offer you a carrier bag to cover your head,' he said, a hint of laugh in his voice.

'Nah, I'm alright, thanks. I just wished I'd parked closer.' She stepped forward triggering the sensor. The door opened and a cold draught slashed across her feet.

'Don't you normally come by underground?'

'I do, but I have a party to go to tonight, so I needed my car. Well, I'm going to brave it, so see you when I see you, Charlie,' she hollered, dashing out of the door into the teeming rain. She held her bag over her head, but it barely covered her fringe. Just as she got to her car parked in a parking lot, she was soaked and shivering. Her phone rang and with shaking hands from the cold she reached into her coat pocket, saw it was her mother calling and put her on speaker while she fumbled in her bag for her car keys.

'Hi mum, I'm just leaving work.' She put the phone on the roof of the car.

'Oh good, so we'll see you in about an hour?'

'Yes, I may take longer if you keep on the phone,' she laughed, pressing the fob.

'Oh right, sorry...'

'Is there something wrong?' She grabbed the phone and pressed it to her ear.

'No, no. I'll see you when you get here, alright; love?'

'Sure? Alright, see you soon.'

The phone clicked on the other end. Holly looked at it confusingly before throwing it on the passenger seat. Whatever could be wrong?' she thought, turning on the ignition.

The traffic was slow and torturous, so she turned up the volume on the radio to destress from work before she entered the crazy house.

About an hour later she had turned into a small suburban street, looking for someplace to park. Thanks to the traffic making her late for the party, her family had arrived before her and had taken up the entire road on either side of the street. She drove along, thinking she got lucky when she found an empty spot, but as she was about to park the car, she realised it was outside old Mrs. Turnbull's residence. Holly grimaced and saw the curtains twitch.

'Still an old bat, I see,' she chuckled to herself and parked the car.

Before she got out of her car, she could hear loud laughter and music from the white 1930's build. Her parent's house was set back from the pavement, surround with thick bushes covered in twinkling lights. She slammed her car door closed, looked up at the house and saw more Christmas lights than Blackpool.

'It never changes.' She shook her despairingly at the sight.

'Alright, Holly,' said a voice in the shadows.

Holly recognised whose choice of cigarettes that she could smell. She hated smoking and the smell was making her retch.

'Oh, it's you, Robert, I suppose you've come for the free food, eh?' she laughed at her brother sitting on the front door step.

'Damn right. You know yourself how far a student loan stretches. Do you know; I survived for four days straight on cheap beans and toast?'

'Let me guess why. You spent the money at the student bar on beer.'

She left him smoking and went inside the house but could barely get through the hallway for people.

'Holly's here,' shouted her cousin Thomas with a can of lager in his hand.

'Thanks, foghorn, I bet they heard that in the next county...'

'You're welcome, and if you're looking for your mother, she's through there,' he pointed towards the kitchen. 'I think she's already drunk on the cider. Mind you, something has been bothering all day, maybe you can find out what it is.'

'Oh okay,' she replied, curious to know what it was, but first she had to find her dad to give him his gift.

'Excuse me,' she asked politely as she made her way through the hallway to the living room that was also crammed full of people. Holly recognised most of the guests as family and the odd neighbour her mother hasn't annoyed in the thirty years they'd lived in Whittlegreen.

Wham's Last Christmas belted out so loud now that nobody could hear her, so she pushed her way through dozens of hellos to find her dad sitting on his favourite armchair with a glass of whiskey in his hand.

'Well, I never,' he jumped up, pulling her in for a hug. 'I didn't think you were coming.' He beamed.

'Happy retirement day, dad,' she hugged him once more, feeling the tackiness of his hair mousse against her cheek. She opened her handbag and took out his present wrapped in Mickey Mouse paper.

'Thanks, Holly,' he frowned at the choice of paper.

'Sorry dad, I was in a rush and the newsagents only had this left. I know you'll like what's inside though. I just hope you haven't got it yet,' she handed him a hardback copy of the latest crime thriller.

'Thanks, Holly,' he enthused, trying to pull off the excessive amount of tape. 'So how have you been?' he asked as someone had taken to the karaoke machine and was singing *Slade's* smash hit.

'I'm okay, we'll talk later, it's your party now so enjoy.'

About to go and find her mother her cousin Sarah appeared out of the crowd and offered her a glass of wine. 'Have a glass or two for me,' she rubbed her swollen belly.

'Thanks, how long left?' she asked with a nod to her bulging stomach.

'Two weeks. I wish it would hurry up though,' she shook her head, exasperated.

'This one is bigger than my other two.'

'Maybe its twins,' she replied noting the terror in Sarah's eyes. 'Rather you than me right now.'

'You don't mean that, once you'll find the right one, before you'll know it, you'll want to settle down and start a family, Holly.'

Not convinced, Holly excused herself and went to find her mother before another relative came to question why she hadn't found anyone to settle down with. After several more "hellos" on her way to the kitchen, she found her mother talking to Scott, her oldest brother by the open back door.

'Alright, mum,' she said.

'Holly, baby, you made it.' She put down her drink and pulled her into an embrace. 'Oh it's nice to see you,' she said, squeezing her tight.

Scott ruffled her hair and went into the living room.

Holly breathed in her mother's favourite scent, Elizabeth Arden and immediately felt at home and relaxed.

'So what was that about in the car?' she asked, picking up a sausage roll from a plate on the kitchen table.

Her mother waved a dismissive hand. 'Later, I'll tell you later when everyone's gone home. Just have a good time now, alright.'

'But...'

'It's nothing wrong in a bad sense,' she leaned in close, whispering. 'It's something I should've given you ages ago that's all.'

'What is it?'

'It's something that Dan left here for you. I only found it this morning when I was cleaning out the cupboards.'

'Really? What is it?'

Her mother took the kitchen towel that was draped over her shoulder and wiped her teary eyes. 'I don't know exactly. It's just a little box. It's upstairs at the moment, so if you want I'll give it to you later when everyone's gone home. I'm sorry, Holly,' her shoulder's shook and she broke down crying.

'Come on, mum, don't be sad, please. It's only now I can talk about him without bursting into tears too.'

'I'm sorry, I didn't mean to upset you, especially tonight...'

Holly felt that it was the wrong time to tell her the news about her work assignment and decided she'd tell them later. Besides, after hearing this, she didn't feel it was right to be happy. 'Do you see me crying over this?' she whispered so nobody else would hear.

Her mother shook her head.

'So don't worry, I don't blame you for forgetting. It means I've got something to look forward to later, eh?'

'What have you got to look forward to?' asked her brother, Scott, walking into the kitchen confounded by the teary looks on the women.

'Oh nothing, honey,' said mum, picking up a bottle of red on the counter and refilling her glass.

Holly jumped in.

'Just having a girly moment, Scott, I'll speak to you later.'

Scott looked at them both curiously and picked up a can of lager off the counter.

'Why are women so secretive?' he shrugged and went back into the living room.

'You can tell why he hasn't found someone to settle with yet, can't you?' Holly chuckled, wondering what her mother had to give her.

STRETCHED OUT ON THE sofa in a drunken stupor, Holly woke and glanced up at the carriage clock on the mantel, noting it was almost 6 a.m. Her father was asleep, snoring on the chair beside the coal fire and her mother was asleep on the sofa next to her sister, Pat. She didn't remember falling asleep or saying goodbye to everyone as they left. Looking at all the glasses and empty bottles on the coffee table she understood why.

She heaved herself from the sofa, thinking she'd make herself a coffee. Careful not to wake everyone, she closed the living room door, almost tumbling over her brother's legs. He was sprawled out in the hallway, sound asleep on the rug. Two beer cans and bowl of pretzels were to his side.

'You silly bugger,' she blurted and covered her mouth, in case anyone else should be in the house sleeping.

Standing by the counter waiting for the kettle to boil, she looked out of the window as the sun started to rise over the park behind the house. The conversation that had taken place with her mother hours earlier floated back into her conscious. She took the biggest mug out of the cupboard and spooned in two sugars wondering what Dan had left with her mother and why.

'Morning,' said Scott, walking into the kitchen. 'I could've sworn somebody smacked me in the legs.' He ruffled his brown hair.

Snapping out of her thoughts, she bid him a good morning and offered to make him a coffee. 'That might've been me, sorry. Next time, before you drink, find somewhere safer to kip.'

'What was going on with you and mam last night?' he asked, yawning, and then stretching out his arms.

Holly remained quiet for a while, and then poured the hot water into the coffee granules.

'Mum said she had something of Dan's here she meant to give me.' She passed him his coffee and sat down at the table opposite him.

'Oh, Holly, I forgot it's been a year already,' he exhaled reaching out a comforting hand across the table. 'Is that what you and mum were talking about last night?'

'Yeah, but I'm... I'm fine with it now, Scott, really fine with it, it's just...'

'You wish you had more time with him, huh?'

She nodded.

'I know I'm not the most sensitive guy and I say things wrong all the time, you can ask Melissa but I'm here for you whenever you need to talk alright? Just give me a holler.'

'I know, and thanks for the talk, it felt good to get it out of the system.'

'Anytime little sister,' he smiled encouragingly and began slurping his coffee.

'Oh, I forgot, I have news. Guess who's writing the Christmas Article?' She grinned, pointing at herself. In all the kerfuffle last night and the mention of Dan, she had spent most of the night thinking of the past. She hadn't even told her parents her big news yet.

'It wouldn't happen to be...*you*, would it?' He grinned.

'It just might be but keep it on the down low. I'd like to tell them both at dinner.'

Chapter Three

The rain lashed against the kitchen window. Holly sat at the table feeling too stuffed to move. Surrounded by dishes of her mother's legendary Sunday roast, she was about to tell her dad her exciting news, but she thought she'd wait until her mother joined them. She even surprised herself at how quiet she has kept and even Scott, who was the biggest blabbermouth she has ever known. About to take a bite out of a stuffing ball, her stomach almost pleaded with her that it couldn't take any more. Reluctantly, she put down her knife and fork when she heard her mother calling her from upstairs.

'Holly,' said her dad, still chewing on a roast potato. 'Your mother is calling you.'

'What is it, mum?' she shouted, getting to her feet. Her stomach felt like a ball of lead.

'Ugh, I think I've eaten too much to move.'

'You'll want to see this,' she shouted back.

Holly climbed the winding staircase, walked across the landing past her old bedroom, to her parent's room facing the back of the house.

She pushed open the half-open door to find her mother bent over, rummaging through her dresser draw.

'Ah, here it is.' She turned to Holly, holding out a small wooden box with a red ribbon on the palm of her hand.

'Is this Dan's Christmas gift?' she asked, about to reach out to take it.

Her mother's face crumpled with anguish. She handed the box over to Holly and sat on the edge of her bed. Holly felt the anxiousness rise.

'When Dan left last Christmas, he gave me this little box to give you as a Christmas gift. It's never been opened, but after what happened to him you were...we all were,' she corrected herself, 'distraught and this completely slipped my mind until yesterday morning. I'm so very sorry, Holly. The last thing I want is for you to be upset, especially with me.'

Close to tears, Holly stared at the box wondering what was inside. She'd only now only come to terms with everything.

'No, I'm not mad at you, mum. It's actually quite nice, it's like he's still with us in a sense. Thanks,' she eventually took the box and held it in her hands. 'Do you know what's in here?'

'No. It's never been opened since the day he brought it around. Look, you don't have to open it now, when you're ready.'

'No, I think you got just as much right to see what's in here,' she smiled, and undid the gold clip. With trepidation, she lifted the lid, surprised to find a gold heart shaped locket cushioned on red velvet lining. On the inside lid of the box, it had an inscription.

To Holly, I love you always,

Dan.

'It's beautiful, mum,' she sniffed back tears.

'Let me see.' Delina took the box with a heavy sigh. 'Will you forgive me for forgetting this?'

Holly threw her arms around her mother, letting her tears spill over her new cashmere jumper.

'Of course, mum, this is the best Christmas present ever.'

'Dan was a great man, Holly,' she patted her back, lovingly while swaying her in her arms.

'He was the best, wasn't he? He can never be replaced.'

Delina broke from the embrace. 'Maybe this isn't the right time to say this, but, you know, there may come a time when you meet someone else, someone just as kind hearted and lovely as Dan...'

'I can't even think of entering a new relationship yet, but I do know what you mean.'

'I don't want to see you alone forever. I worry about you over in that little flat by yourself. Please, don't close your heart. Dan wouldn't want that.'

'I suppose you're right. But there's no need to worry because I won't be home next week.'

'Oh?'

Holly closed the lid on the box. 'Mum, I have something exciting I've been meaning to talk to you and dad about since I got here.'

'What is it?'

'Hang on...' she jumped off the bed and went out onto the landing. 'Dad, come up here a second, will you.'

Holly heard him mumble something incoherently and went back into the room.

'What is it?' he asked standing by the bedroom door.

'I've been asked to write the Christmas feature for the newspaper.'

Delina clasped her hands over her mouth in shock.

'Have you really?'

Holly nodded with a smile.

'That's bloody fantastic,' shouted her dad who came over to give her a hug.

'I'm going to Snowdonia to write about their Christmas village. I didn't even know they had one. Isn't it exciting?'

Delina wiped her eyes with her sleeve and began jumping up and down. She took hold of Holly by the arms.

'That is the best news, Holly, come on, we've got to go and tell everyone in my phone contacts. Oh and remind me to update my Facebook status as well.'

ONCE HER MOTHER HAD calmed down and had finished calling all of her friends with the news that her daughter was now a real journalist, Holly went into the conservatory for a little down time.

'Mind if I use your laptop, mum? I left mine at home,' Holly asked.

'Sure love,' she yelled from the kitchen. 'Are you doing research for your article?'

'Yeah, I'm so excited,' she picked up the laptop from the coffee table and sat down on the sofa. She had no idea where to start, or what she was going to write about. In the search bar she typed *"Christmas Village, Snowdonia,"* and saw at the top of the screen, an advert for a Christmas weekend away for their Winterfest.

'Mmm,' she thought about researching the history of the village and covering the infamous Winterfest. Tapping a pen at the side of her cheek, she decided to find one resident with a unique story to tell instead.

'Found anything to write about?' asked her mum walking through the living room with a tray of tea and cake.

'Not sure. What do you know about this Christmas Village? I can't say I've heard of it but sounds like fun. Maybe there'll be tons of stories from people who love Christmas I could write about.'

Her mother looked at the screen. 'Never heard of it before, but like I always told you, if you got a hunch, go for it…'

'I think I will.' She read the article, intrigued, almost captivated by the place. 'I'm going to confirm my hotel room.'

Later that evening, after another round of leftover lunch, she said goodbye to her parents standing on the doorstep and got into her car.

'I'll call you when I'm in Snowdonia,' she waved back through the passenger window.

'You be careful on them roads, you hear me?' said her father. 'You may want to consider getting a decent car first before you go.'

She gave him the thumbs up and clipped her belt, feeling glum about going back to her tiny flat. The forty-five-minute journey to the city passed by quickly as she sat thinking about the party and the locket, but as soon she arrived at the block of flats she didn't want to go inside. Slipping the key in her lock, she pushed open the door and dumped her bags on the floor.

'Home sweet home, Holly,' she grimaced and went into her tiny kitchen to make a cup of tea.

The morning of her trip, Holly woke to the sound of her alarm, dragged herself out of bed and went into the kitchen. After she had flicked the kettle on, she then picked up the television remote on the counter, pointed it towards her television in the living room and switched it on. Almost instantly she regretted the decision. Part of her didn't know why she did it in the first place as she barely watched it; preferring her ever growing TBR pile on her Kindle. But when the news came on about a bomb attack in Lebanon, killing hundreds she couldn't pull herself away, thinking herself bad if she did. She always did have a kooky way of looking at things, but that's what made her unique as Daniel always told her so. Ah, *Daniel*. How she missed him. The apartment is freezing since she hadn't put the heating on, so she sat down on the sofa, hands cupped around her steaming hot mug of coffee as the report unpicked battle wounds of her own. She shook her head at the television screen and then reached to her handbag lain on the glass table, pulling out a packet of cigarettes. She had given them up days ago, promising she'd have a new healthier lifestyle, but found herself unconsciously pulling one out of the packet. Force of habit, she muttered, but refused to put it back.

It was now 4.45 a.m. and she was already dressed and anxious to go, she wondered if *she* had gone mad or the world that she lived in. She placed it between her lips, lit it; and took in a long, slow drag, figuring maybe both, but at least she wasn't the one killing innocent people. To her relief, the news finally followed the weather, and she looked over her shoulder, towards the window. Between the slacks of the blind, rain fell hard in the orange beam of the streetlight.

'Bloody great,' she muttered, thinking she ought to get her suitcase packed and, in the car, ready for the long drive to Snowdonia.

Sifting through her wardrobe for jumpers to pack her phone pinged with several notifications. She picked it up from her dresser, seeing a message from Emily.

Hope you find the story you're looking for.

Thanks, Em. I'll let you know as soon as I do.

She returned to the wardrobe and the task at hand, grabbed the first few jumpers on her shelf and tossed them into her case, along with a few pairs of jeans and the thickest socks she owned. Satisfied she had enough to see through two days, she was about to head out of the room, when her eye caught the box given to her by her mother stopped her in her tracks.

Part of her wanted to cry and crawl back to bed, but she had been healing over the last few months and didn't want to go back to the horrible three months when she couldn't leave the flat. Carefully, she picked it up, opened the lid and took it out of the box. But her emotions got the best of her, and she clenched the necklace in her hands as tears rolled down her cheeks. She sat down on her bed, crying until she couldn't cry anymore. 'I think I'm going to take you with me,' she whispered. She put on the necklace, sure to tuck it safe under her black fuzzy jumper. This way, she thought, he would be with her as a good luck charm.

'Gosh, I miss you Dan,' she sniffed, pressing a hand to her chest.

She took a few moments to allow it all to sink in, and then headed for her bedroom door. Snatching her phone from the dresser, she caught her reflection in the mirror. Her dark hair was tied into a messy bun and no matter how long she sunbathed for, she always looked pale, not that it bothered her so much. It was a great asset to have when she went through her Gothic phase at college, but nowadays she thought she just looked anaemic. She figured she needed a little colour and delved into her make-up bag.

Holly couldn't decide on the bronzer or blusher, and after a little deliberation she figured she could use both. She grabbed her make-up bag, threw it into her suitcase and hauled her luggage out into the living room.

Chapter Four

' *Country road, take me home,*' she sang, driving along the narrow, windy country road. The music blared, and the window was open wide, but she didn't care. Despite her lack of singing talent, there was nobody around for miles. The last car she saw was about two hours ago at the services stop. She took in a lungful of the fresh, crisp autumn air and relaxed back into the seat. For the first time in months, she felt calm and more like her old self. It was as though the emotional baggage she had carried for so long seemed to have drifted away since being in close proximity to nature. There was something magical about this time of year, she thought, turning the radio down a few notches. Ahead of her, the sun hung low in the sky; its light filtering through the golden leaves of the trees that bordered her path to the Christmas Village, a village she had never heard of until a couple of days ago. She checked the dashboard for the time and groaned. If it hadn't been for leaving so late and the flat tyre she'd have been there by now.

Bloody car, she cussed, frustrated after leaving so early this morning. She tapped the steering wheel along to the song when something flew past her line of vision, taking her by surprise. She flinched, momentarily losing control of the car.

'Oh my God,' she screamed.

The car swerved to the side, hitting a few stray branches, and narrowly missing the ditch. Her heart pounded as she quickly took back control and wound-up the window.

'Jeez, Holly, get a grip – it was just a moth,' she sighed, grabbing a peppermint from the packet on the passenger seat. She laughed at her silliness, thinking she'd better get used to it having to spend a weekend in the countryside.

Gradually, it got darker, until there was nothing but the beam of the headlights in front of her.

Tiredness now setting in, she yawned and glanced at the sat nav. According to her new device, she only had half of mile to go, and could feel her eyelids drooping at a scary rate. 'You've got to stay awake, Holly, you can do this,' she said, now determined to get to her destination. She switched the radio on to something more upbeat as the road opened out to fields on either side.

As soon as the song ended, the clear starlit sky and the tip of a mountain with the moonlight reflecting on snow appeared like a vision before her eyes.

'Wow.' She leaned forward of the seat, mesmerised by the scene in front of her. 'Woah, this place looks like it's jumped out of a Christmas card.' She made a mental note to snap a picture for her mother on the way home and carried on driving.

She slowed down, parking the car on the side of the road and opened her glove box. She *was* in the right place, wasn't she? She was about to go through her phone for her email confirmation when a bright set of car headlights came around the bend almost blinding her. She covered her eyes with the back of her hand, cursing the bloody driver. The vehicle slowed to a stop in front of her car and she opened her door to investigate.

'It's okay, I've not broken down, but thanks for stopping,' she said to the silhouetted figure approaching her. She regretted getting out of the car and began to panic, thinking he could be a rapist, or a murderer or both. Slowly slipping her hand into her jacket pocket, she took out her phone ready to dial 999. If there was ever anyone to blame for her cautiousness, it was her father who was now an ex-chief of police.

'Oh, I'm sorry,' said a rather handsome, but apologetic voice. 'It looked like you have.'

He stepped in front of the lights and she quickly took a mental note of what he was wearing. She couldn't see much, but noticed he wore a hat, glasses, denims and a pair of trainers. Yes, she never missed a trick.

Holly relaxed, slightly taken aback by how classically beautiful he was and stuffed the phone into her pocket. 'I just stopped to check my map. I'm really sorry for the bother.'

He smiled. 'No bother. Could I be of help and direct you?' He asked, rubbing his hands together for warmth.

Relieved he didn't seem like a monster; Holly took out her phone but the battery died on her.

'Bugger, there's no signal, give me a moment.'

Remembering she had printed out the hotels' website, she opened her door and reached over the seat for the folded piece of paper. 'I'm looking for this place, would you know it?' she asked handing it to him as he came forward. She caught a whiff of his scent which reminded her of her Dan. He'd always wear on the rare occasions he was home from the army. The woody, masculine smell also made her think of the woods surrounding them.

'Uh, let's see,' he said, moving towards the car headlights to get a better look.

Holly felt awkward by the handsome stranger's face so close to hers as he studied the paper in front of him. She also noted his strong hands and the silver rings he wore. And was there a small tattoo the side of his finger? Engrossed in her own thoughts she didn't hear him the first time when he called her.

'Um, miss?' he said.

'Oh, sorry, miles away,' she replied, snapping out of her thoughts.

'It's okay. This is Christmas Village, so you're their new guest?' He handed the papers back to her. 'They were expecting some woman hours ago...'

'I am their guest, yep. So you know of it?'

He found her response funny. 'Of course, follow me. I'll show you the way.'

'Are you sure, it looks like you're going that way?' she thumbed behind her.

'It's okay; I was only going for a late night drivel.' He turned around to get back into his car, but paused by the door and looked back at her. 'So what's your name if you don't mind me asking?'

'What's yours?' she asked cheekily.

He laughed.

'Benjamin, but you can call me Ben.'

Holly stuck out her hand. 'Nice to meet you, Ben, I'm Holly.' She shook his hand and then got back into her car.

Chapter Five

She waited for him to swerve his car around so she could start following his lead. Yet, it wasn't until she started driving, she realised it wasn't the way in which she was intentionally headed. There was a fork in the road and although her satellite navigation said to take the left, he took the right. Her heart thumped madly, and her hands sweated on the steering wheel. She could hardly turn back now, or could she? He turned another bend in the road when Holly noticed tiny specks of snow landing on her windshield.

She gasped.

'Bloody hell, it's actually snowing here,' she shrieked excitedly, momentarily forgetting the situation at hand. A gust of wind blew the snow in the direction of the trees to her left; revealing small cottages with thatched roofs along the roadside. She stared in awe as she passed and then drew her attention back to the road she was on. In the frame of the windshield, on the opposite side of the road, a large board with *You're Now Entering Christmas Village*, came into view. She relaxed her hands on the steering wheel, relieved he'd been truthful with her.

The road led her to a quaint village with Edwardian frontage shops. Their bay, lattice windows were painted red and green, and the doors were already decorated with Christmas wreaths and lights. The picturesque scene stirred emotions inside of her she hadn't felt for a long time.

Unable to take her eyes from the passenger window; she didn't notice a car that was pulling out. The driver beeped its horn, snapping her attention back to her driving. Holly slammed on the breaks before she almost smacked into Ben's bumper.

'That was close,' she mumbled to herself.

Her car spluttered and cut out. She turned the ignition again, her fingers shaking with the cold. After three tries, she gave up, defeated and wishing she'd bought a Land Rover.

Ben got out of his car, holding his arm above his eyes to shield off the heavy snow flurries. She rolled down her window.

'It won't start.'

'I didn't think your car would've made it up that hill without chains anyway, so I think it's best if you leave it here and let me give you a lift.' He said, genuinely happy, despite the sudden cold snap and the heavy snow fall.

Realising she didn't have much choice, she agreed. 'If it's no trouble,' she got out of the car, her boots hitting the slush. She surveyed her surroundings, counting at least twenty shops with a public square and the tallest Christmas tree she'd ever seen lovingly placed in the centre. Even in the fading twilight, it looked magical lit up with multi-coloured lights.

'This is just the town, the place you're staying is up on that hill,' he pointed. 'So come on, give me a hand to get the car to the kerb and I'll get a mechanic to come and take a look at it for you.'

'Are you sure?'

'Of course, glad to help.'

Holly got back into the driver's seat to steer the car while Ben pushed it outside a coffee shop. After locking the side doors and checking she hadn't left anything, she got her handbag and went to collect her bags from the boot.

'Here, let me help you,' he took her bags.

'Thanks, so have you lived here long?'

'Yes, all my life. Wouldn't want to live anywhere else,' he said, closing her passenger side door as he passed. 'Allow me.' He bundled her luggage in his left hand, and with his free hand he opened his passenger door for her.

The warmth of the car was welcomed as she slammed the door shut on the cold. She shivered, rubbing her numb hands. She hadn't known cold like this before.

'Are you cold? He asked, closing his door.

'I'm freezing. I wasn't expecting anything like this,' she raised a gloved hand to indicate the weather outside.

'No? What did you expect, sandy beaches and Californian sunshine? So where are you from then?' He started the car. 'You're obviously not from these parts.'

'No. Just outside of London, but I live in the city now for work.'

'So you've had a long drive today, I take it. And you're staying at the Gingerbread Log Cabin, right?'

'I am, and did you say log cabins?'

'Yeah I did, why? Did you think it was a hotel?'

'Yeah, I did. I must've stupidly mistaken the main picture to be one place. Anyway, it looked so sickly sweet. I can imagine people sleepwalking, trying to eat it,' she laughed and then stopped short when she thought she may have offended him, or worse. What if he thought she was a bit on the nutty side?

Besides, she couldn't afford to upset any of the locals just yet, not when she needed to get them on her side.

Holly cleared her throat, a little embarrassed.

'I know what you mean, but the tourists love it, especially the Americans and Japanese that come over here.'

He drove the steep ascent until it levelled off on to a flat road. Holly looked around. 'Where are the log cabins then?'

Ben pointed to the left. 'It's just up here, tucked away. The log cabins go back as far as the mountainside though. So what brings you to here then, holiday?'

'Oh gosh, no, I'm here for work. I'm a journalist, looking to do a feature story on one of the residents.'

Ben laughed. 'Well good luck with that one, then. I'm not saying the people aren't accommodating, it's just...'

Anxious rising, Holly faced him. 'What?'

'They don't take too kindly to people nosing in their business. I'm sure you wouldn't like that either...'

'Well, no, but it's not going to be a demeaning article. Have you heard of the newspaper called *The World*?'

'Yeah, I've heard of it, who hasn't?'

'Well, every Christmas Eve it publishes a Christmas themed article that's supposed to invoke the Christmas spirit in people. It has even won awards.'

'I'm writing it this year.'

'Are you really?' He blurted, genuinely surprised. 'So I have a celebrity in my car then, wow.'

Holly's heart did a little leap with joy that he knew of the newspaper, but then, who didn't.

'I'm hardly a celebrity, thanks. In fact I don't think I'd want to be one. On a serious note though, I reckon the article could help boost business here. It has happened before.' She saw him frown at her words. 'Oh I don't mean that it needs it, but hey, who can turn their nose up at extra business?'

'Yes, I see your point.'

'I'm quite confident that it'll put The Christmas Village on the map for sure.'

Ben nodded his response. Holly could only guess at what he was thinking. She hoped people would be welcoming of her and not make her job too difficult.

'Okay, you've got me intrigued. I hope you find what you're looking for here.'

'Thanks, your support is most welcomed,' she laughed.

THE CAR SLOWED DOWN. Holly rubbed the condensation on the window and looked outside. In amongst the snow flurries she could make out lights in windows filtering through the snowy branches of the trees.

'Are we here?' she asked, realising she sounded like an excited child.

'We are most definitely here,' he drove to the large, wooden gates that swung open when he approached.

The main building was a two-storey cabin and scattered around the snowy landscape were smaller cabins, their windows lit with a warm glow. She sat up in her seat just as a black cat jumped out of the snow pile on the side of the driveway, dashing across the road.

'This place can't be real. Am I dreaming?' she turned to Ben, smiling widely.

'I hope not. I've lived here almost all my life. Wait until morning; when you'll see it in all its splendour, you're going to love it.'

Her cheeriness drooped.

'Well, I hope so. To be honest, I lost my Christmas spirit a long time ago.' She shrugged, clutching her handbag to her chest.

Ben laughed.

'And you're writing *the* most anticipated article of the year? Anyway, I wouldn't go around saying that to anyone here either.'

'What if I happened to let it slip?'

'Honey, you're in Christmas Village where Christmas is twenty-four hours a day, seven days a week and fifty-two weeks of the year. Let's face it; you've got to love it to endure it for *that* long. And if you don't love it, they'll know and do their damnedest to convince you otherwise.'

Holly laughed.

'And do you love it?'

'Hey, I was born here, it's not like I had a choice in the matter.'

'I promise I won't say anything to offend Christmas. So what do you do here?'

Ben's face became serious. 'At the moment I'm helping out my dad with his business,' he replied, vaguely. 'Oh, and here we are,' he said, pulling up outside the cabin.

'So this is the place, eh? Thanks for all your help, I really appreciate it.'

'Don't mention it. And I'll get Stanley to look at your car first thing.'

'Thank you, you've been so kind.'

'Don't mention my kindness to anyone or they will all take advantage,' he joked.

She unclipped her belt, got out of the car and went to the boot to retrieve her luggage. Ben also got out of the car, and as she walked towards the cabin, she could hear Benjamin's feet on snow following behind her. After all his help, she didn't feel like telling him to bugger off and leave her alone. In some small way she was glad of the company right now. Someone to share in her joy of finally getting a wish ticked off on her list. That she was now a proper journalist. He now stood to her side.

'So have you any idea what kind of story you're after?' he asked.

'Well... truthfully, I don't know. I guess I will know when I find it.'

'I have to be honest. I sort of knew there would be a journalist coming here and I knew you weren't her when I met you. Apparently, she had been phoning every business in town asking questions before she even got here, so I knew you weren't her. I actually spoke with her myself.'

Holly stood in the beams of the car headlights and pursed her lips. She broke eye contact with Ben and looked towards the darkness feeling a little cheated that he knew about her arrival. But then she had another thought. What if he was part of the story the other woman was writing about?

'Wow, you kept that one quiet. So, this makes me wonder if Felicity had found a potential story in you.' She then looked up at him beaming at her. 'But you're absolutely right. I haven't got a clue what I'm doing here.' She laughed. 'I guess I'll have to wing it.'

'I think you'll do okay,' he said, carrying her bags up the wooden steps to the door.

Holly rang the doorbell and wasn't surprised to hear Jingle Bells. She thought back to the day at the office and smiled to herself as there was no escaping the song this time of year.

'Susan is really nice, so is her husband Clive. They've run this place for the last twenty years or so. So, if you want to know anything, these folks are the ones to ask.'

Holly looked through the snowflake frosted glass door and saw the silhouette of a woman about to open the door.

'Thanks for the tip, so...I'll see you around?'

Ben put down her bags.

'Of course, if you're around town give me a holler, goodnight, Holly. It was nice to meet you.'

The door opened and a pool of light cascaded down the steps. A tall woman with bobbed blonde hair greeted her with a warm smile. She rolled up the sleeves of her grey knitted jumper and proffered her hand.

'Hello, you must Miss Green?' She saw Ben about to leave and waved him to stop. 'Did you want something, Ben?'

'No, I found Holly out on the main road into the place, so I directed her to town and then her car broke down so I gave her a lift.'

'That's nice of you, love. See you tomorrow.' She waved.

'No problem, Sue. She was looking like a lost sheep so I could hardly leave her stranded in this cold.' He winked at Holly.

Holly gushed thinking he had a gorgeous smile.

'So, Holly; how was your trip?' she asked, holding the door open for her. 'We did get a bit worried as we were expecting you hours ago.'

'Long and tiring,' she replied, looking around the lobby with the wonder of a child. 'I'm sorry I couldn't call; the signal has been on and off all the way here.' She stood by the oak reception desk and put down her bags. A seven-foot Christmas tree with shiny, golden baubles stood next to the window. Not even the small town she lived in could afford a tree that size. The one they had was about her height, five foot four and looking sparse, thanks to the local youths nicking the baubles every night. 'You have a beautiful place, so festive. I take it's like this all year around?'

'It is,' replied Susan, now behind the desk going through her bookings log. 'Ah, here you are, Holly Green, correct?'

'Yes.'

'That's quite a festive name you have, too.'

'So I've been told,' she smiled tightly and then rolled her eyes at the woman when she looked down at her book again.

'Well, as we've had a cancellation, I can offer you our best cabin on the block, no extra charge. Follow me.'

'Oh lovely,' she said, picking up her luggage. 'I have to admit, I thought this was a hotel before I got here.' She followed Susan to the main door.

'We have log cabins. I'm sure you'd appreciate it a lot more than a regular hotel room.'

'I'm sure I will.'

'Oh you were lucky he found you,' she said leading her across the snow covered field to a wooden cabin nestled under snow covered trees.

'I am lucky,' she replied, trying to keep up with her. 'Though I do have to admit as first I thought he was going to try something funny.'

Susan laughed. 'Gosh, no, love. Ben is the nicest guy you could ever wish to meet. If anyone should've found you tonight, thank your lucky stars it was him. He knows this place like the back of his hand.' She slipped the key into the lock and pushed open the door. 'Here you go,' she gestured Holly inside. 'I hope you like your home from home for a while.'

Holly stepped inside, taken aback at how cosy and Christmassy it felt. A red tartan blanket draped over the luxurious king-size bed beside the window framed with the snowy woods. To the right there were a small makeshift kitchen and a log fire already cackling.

'Here's your key. We also have a restaurant over the main cabin if you fancy a change from cooking for yourself. Or I can recommend Betty's café in town.'

'Thank you, this is gorgeous,' she beamed, casting her eyes around the room.

Chapter Six

She woke on her bed, cuddled under the duvet, listening to the sound of the birds outside her window. She thought it made a refreshing change from the traffic she'd get outside her flat. Once she was fully awake, she pushed herself up against the headboard, shivering.

'Jeez, it's cold here.'

The alarm she set for eight hadn't yet gone off, so she stayed for a while and scrolled through her phone. There was a message from her dad asking if she wanted to spend Christmas with them for a change and he hoped she wouldn't be a miser again this year with no tree.

'Thanks for that, dad and okay, I'll be home late afternoon on Christmas Eve,' she typed back. 'And this year, I may surprise you.' She added a laughing emoticon at the end of the message and sent it.

'And before I forget,' he replied instantly, 'I hope you have a nice time, send us a postcard.'

Holly laughed.

'It may be quicker to snap you a picture.'

She slipped her foot out of her blanket and immediately drew it back. It was freezing since she allowed the fire to go out. She reached out a hand to the floor, snatched her fuzzy socks and slipped them on. There was no point staying in bed, as much as she'd love to. The article wasn't going to write itself. Her stomach growled reminding her she hadn't ate anything since she arrived.

Be brave, Holly and throw the damn covers off.

She shivered uncontrollably and cursed the fact she didn't put the logs on the fire. She threw open the suitcase and rummaged through piles of creased clothes for a jumper. Under a heap of bra's she found the one decent jumper she owned and pulled it on. She heard a vehicle approaching her cabin and looked at the clock. It wasn't even eight yet, so who could it be? In fact, who knew she was here. She rushed to the window but couldn't see who was outside. The car door closed followed by a knock at the front door. She looked down at her PJ bottoms thinking it was best to change them and grabbed her jeans slung over a box by her bed.

'Coming,' she yelled, buttoning up her jeans. She rushed to the door, undid the latch and then the lock, sure to keep the chain on and yanked the door open. A man stood on the porch with a big, cheesy grin.

'Morning, I hope it was okay to pop by at such a ghastly hour,' said Benjamin holding two red paper cups with a white plastic lid.

It took her a few moments to think who he was. Her mind ticked back to last night and to the handsome stranger that came to her rescue.

'Oh, it's you,' she said, almost kicking herself at how rude she sounded. 'Sorry, I didn't mean it like that.' She closed the door, cussed under her breath and slipped off the chain.

'I didn't mean to come unannounced. After last night, I just wanted to check that you were okay and if you needed anything.'

She noticed his eye colour now, as he wasn't wearing his glasses. They were pale blue that contrasted beautifully with his dark hair sticking out from under his grey beanie.

'Where's my manners, come in, you must be freezing.' She stepped back and held the door open. Before he came in, he handed her a coffee.

'I took a chance. If you're one of those very rare people who don't like the stuff, I won't be offended.'

Grateful, she took the warm coffee that felt great against her cold skin and looked down at her green fluffy slippers. At least she had the good sense to get dressed.

'I'm not a big fan of the stuff, but thank you, anyway.' She took him through to the kitchen and offered him a stool to sit on next to the island. 'So, it's Benjamin, isn't it?' She said, removing the coffee lid.

His eyes lit up.

'I'm surprised you remembered.'

'I'm very good at remembering names and faces. I have my dad to blame for that,' she said.

His eyes narrowed. 'Oh?'

'Policeman's daughter,' she chuckled into her drink.

'Ah, well you'll be glad to know I don't even have a record.' He lifted his cup as if to say cheers and took a sip of his coffee.

'So what exactly do you do around here if you don't mind me asking?' She leant back against the sink and glanced up at the clock, thinking she ought to get into town as soon as possible.

'Why do I get the feeling I've come at the wrong time. Do you want me to leave?'

'No,' she spluttered on her coffee. 'No, I'm sorry. I've only just got up and I need to get into town.' She sipped her coffee once again and then put the cup on the counter. It was eight-fifteen. 'Well, not at this exact moment as I don't have a car.'

'Late riser, I see. Sorry, Holly, it's just that I knew I'd be passing, so I thought I'd be a good sport and bring you a welcoming coffee.'

'Passing...with coffee?' She raised an eyebrow in suspicion. 'That's very convenient, don't you think?'

Ben blushed.

'Um, yeah, not entirely true, I'm afraid. You got me there.' There was a slight, awkward pause. 'So what are you hoping to uncover today? A deep, dark secret that will threaten the town...'

'No, nothing that dramatic, but it would make for good reading. I need a heartfelt story, something that people will care about. The only trouble is; I have to write ten thousand words by the twentieth. If I don't get it, I can kiss goodbye to a career in proper journalism, and I'll be writing the agony aunt section for the rest of my life.'

Benjamin had a smirk on his face. 'I'm sure it won't come to that. Listen do you want me to give you a tour of the place? I really don't mind.'

Holly thought he was a little too keen but seemed harmless enough so agreed. 'Alright then, let me grab my coat.'

'Oh and Stan said he's going to take a look at your car later this afternoon, so it should be ready for you by tomorrow evening.'

'I really appreciate it, thanks,' she said pulling on her hat.

Chapter Seven

Her foot sunk into the freezing cold snow, soaking the bottom of her jeans. 'Gosh, it did come down heavily last night, didn't it?' She cast her eyes down the patchwork valley, at the white topped hills dotted with small farmhouses.

Ben held out his hand. 'Want a hand down the slope?'

'I'm good thanks. I brought my snow boots.'

Ben looked down to her feet and let out a laugh, shaking his head in amusement at her choice of footwear, a pair of purple Dr Martens.

'Well, you may want to attach a pair snow grips to them,' he joked. 'This stuff is lethal if you're not used to it.'

Holly waved a hand to dismiss the comment. 'I'll be alright...' just as she took one step forward, she realised the enormity of the task ahead. 'This stuff is tough to walk in.'

'Here,' he offered a gloved hand once more. 'Take my hand, I don't bite.'

'Okay, thanks. Just until we...' she reached out her hand and fell forward. Ben swooped in, catching her before she hit the ground. He held her a few seconds longer than she thought necessary but that was only to make sure she was steady her on her feet. Holly looked up and as she he did, their eyes locked for a few brief seconds, long enough to make her blush with embarrassment.

'How can you stand this cold?' she asked, deliberately looking away and changing the conversation.

'Thermal underwear.'

Holly laughed.

'Serious?'

Ben gazed down at her with his chocolate eyes, the curves of his lips rising. 'Of course, I'm willing to bet if you ask anyone here how they get through the winters they'll say it's thermal underwear. You may want to consider buying some.'

'Three layers of t-shirts under a thick woollen jumper are doing me just fine for now.'

'I'll bet you dinner at The Lodge that come Sunday you'll be at The Mill for thermal underwear.'

Holly laughed hard. Was he asking her out to dinner? Thinking he was joking, she decided to call his bluff. 'Okay, it's a done deal. If, come Sunday and I'm still here and I am caught buying thermal underwear, then I'll buy the dinner *and* a desert.'

'I'm holding you to that. I know the guy who works there, a buddy of mine, so you won't get away with this.'

'Alright, I bet I could go in there, buy a thermal vest and you wouldn't be none the wiser.'

They'd reached the bottom of the hill and stood beside the roadside, next to a pile of brown slush snow.

'Now you're getting serious.'

'I never lose a bet.'

Ben tossed his keys. 'We'll see.' He opened the truck door for her and gestured her inside.

'Thank you.' She got into the passenger side, surprised how happy she felt. Less than twenty-four hours ago she was having second thoughts about coming. And if she didn't come, she wouldn't have met Ben. She reminded herself that the sole reason she was here was to find a story, so that meant business. As soon as Ben had got into the driver's side she snapped into her journalist persona she had spent years perfecting in her mirror. Whilst some girls held a brush practicing to sing, Holly spent her teenage years holding a brush pretending to interview the pop stars of the day.

'So tell me a bit about you and this place?'

Ben put the keys into the ignition. 'All in good time, honey. Tell me more about you. Why did you choose to come to this place anyhow?'

'It wasn't actually me; it was the other journalist that chose it. If she was reachable by phone, I'd know what story she was looking to cover. It'd make my job easier that's for sure.'

He chuckled.

'Honestly? It sounds like you didn't get a say in the matter then. But look at it this way, if you followed her story, it wouldn't be yours now, would it?'

'I guess you have a point there. Well, I've got one more day, so wish me luck. Actually,' she faced him. 'You wouldn't have any idea where I could start?' she jokingly fluttered her lashes hoping he would give her a little nudge in the right direction.

Ben opened his mouth to speak but then shook his head.

'Do you know what? Perhaps it'll be better if you found it. It will make it more special then, wouldn't it?'

Holly thought for a moment. 'Yeah, I agree. I came here thinking I needed to find her story, but this is my show now. Thanks.'

'You're very welcome.'

They were driving along a country road when the trees became less until there were rows of shops. Strings of coloured lights wrapped in lush green garland topped with snow hung across the road with a large banner welcoming everyone to this year's Winterfest.

Holly wound the window down and took out her camera. 'It's like something from a Hallmark movie.' She gushed, snapping away at the quaint shops.

'They've made a few here, mind you. So where would you like to visit first?'

'Don't you have work to go to?'

'I do in a little while but let me introduce you to some people first.'

'Do all the newcomers get this treatment, I wonder?'

'Only some,' he winked and parked the car against the kerb. 'And I'll check on Stan at the garage for you later. Hopefully he won't be too long with your car.'

'That's so kind of you, thank you.'

She got out of the car into the shivering cold wondering how the shoppers all had smiles on their faces, but even she had to agree, the place had an aura of wonderment and magic about it. Although she wrote for a living, even she couldn't articulate her thoughts on how she felt, except at ease and excited for the first time in a long time.

'So where are we going?'

'In here,' he pointed to a shop with lattice windows covered with fake snow, not that it needed the fake snow. There was enough of the white stuff for miles.

'It's Betty's Diner, you'll love it. All the local gossips hang around here, so I say it's the best place to start. Plus she makes the best milkshakes.'

'Are you having one, I mean a tea, or a coffee?'

He was about to answer when his mobile rang. 'Excuse me a moment.'

Holly nodded, then turned towards the shop and noticed a sign on the door. She stepped closer to get a better look.

SAVE THE CHRISTMAS TREE FARM. SIGN THE PETITION

The moment she read it she knew she had her story and was eager to enter the shop. About to push the door open, Ben had got off his phone, striding towards her.

'I'm sorry, Holly, Dad needs me at work. Maybe I'll meet you later on. Do you want to swap numbers?' he asked. 'Because if the car isn't finished, I'm guessing you'll need a lift back to the hotel.'

'Sure,' she took his phone and punched in her number. 'No worries. There's plenty here to keep me occupied for the day.'

'Alright then, well... don't forget our bet.'

'I won't, and thank you for the lift and the coffee.'

'My pleasure.'

Walking backwards to his car, he waved, seemingly reluctant to leave. It wasn't until he crashed into his car; he blushed and opened the door to make a quick exit. Holly chuckled as she entered the shop into a concoction of coffee and baked goods, hardly believing how easy her job had been. Now all she had to do was find out the details, snap a few pictures and she had her article. Except, she had a niggling feeling it was all too easy.

'Hello,' she said to the woman behind the counter who was decorating a sponge cake with icing. The woman with blonde hair tied back into a ponytail looked up. 'Could I have a tea please?' she asked, removing her gloves.

'You certainly can, love. Here for a spot of Christmas shopping, are you?'

'Yeah, I got here last night. It's a gorgeous place, can't believe I've never heard of it until recently.'

'Well, we're not one to boast, but yes it's gorgeous,' she laughed. 'So can I get you anything with the tea?'

'I'll have a slice of fruit cake, thanks,' she asked,

The café was full of people, mainly families sitting in the classic red backed booths. The jukebox belted out Jingle Bell Rock.

'I'll fetch it to your table if you want,' she said.

Holly notices her wreath shaped name tag.

'Thank you, Betty,' she looked around for an empty seat, but decided to sit beside the bar.

'What's happening with the Christmas Tree Farm?' she handed her change.

Betty sighed deeply. 'You don't know of it, do you?'

Holly shook her head.

'Well, the town was built around the farm many years ago,' she handed her the tea. 'The owner, Alfred and his son just found out the farm was leasehold and the owner of said leasehold is threatening to sell it if they can't come up with a hundred grand by Christmas Eve. Actually, from what I heard today there is no hope and papers will be signed.'

'That's awful,' she took a sip of her tea. 'I take it by the sign in the window they can't afford that, huh?'

'No. If that place goes, so does the heart of the town.'

'That's bad...'

Thinking she ought to stop interrogating the woman, Holly thanked her for her tea and spotted an empty seat beside the window. She opened her bag, took out her notebook and started to write notes.

Despite what Ben had told her, she was going ahead with her plans to write the story. There was no way they could refuse the much-needed publicity. Could they? She began writing, hoping the residents would be on her side.

'

Chapter Eight

Armed with her story, Holly felt quite pleased with herself as she left the café. She took a casual stroll up the street, browsing in the shop windows, wondering if it was the same story the other journalist had picked up on. She sent the woman another message and walked through an open shop door. She never expected find a story so quickly and so decided she was going to make the most of her couple of days away. She texted Emily

Found the story.

A few seconds later a reply came through.

That quick! Does it involve a sexy man?

Holly laughed, thinking of Ben.

No, well, maybe. I'll tell you more when I'm back in my cabin.

'Can I help you?' asked a short, elderly man wearing a red apron behind the counter.

Holly stuffed her phone in her pocket, realising she was standing in a toy store full of old, wooden traditional toys.

'Wow,' she gushed. 'This is amazing. Do you make these?'

'Used to, but now my son has taken over the business. I just run the front of shop these days. Helps with the arthritis,' he chuckled.

'I don't blame you; I'd love to work in a place like this. I bet it's a great feeling when the kids come in here and they leave happy with their toys. Hey, you could be the village's Santa Claus.'

The man's cheeks flushed red. 'I wish I was love, but no, there's one of those.' He patted the side of his nose with a finger. 'Are you looking for anything in particular or are you just browsing?'

'Well now I'm here, I was wondering if you could tell me how you feel about the tree farm that's closing down.'

'Oh?' He frowned.

'Sorry, I'm Holly Green from *The World* newspaper. I'm writing the Christmas article this year and I've decided to try and help the farm.'

'Well that's mighty good of you. So let's see,' he pondered. 'What can I tell you? You know, if that place goes under, we all do. I'm not sure how much old Harry needs, but I know the man doesn't have that kind of money lying around.'

'Must've took you all by surprise when you heard, huh?'

'Oh gosh, yes. But no more than poor, Harry. He thought he owned the place outright, can you imagine the shock of receiving a legal letter saying you have until Christmas Eve to find a load of cash or we'll take your business from you.'

'Gosh, that's awful. Would you mind if I quote you in the article, Mister...?

'Sandleson. And of course; I'll do anything to help.'

'Thank you,' she took her notebook out of her pocket and scribbled down what he had said. 'Thank you, again. Would you mind directing me to the farm?'

'Sure, love. You go out here, walk to the top of this road, take a left down the country road and you can't miss it.'

'Thank you for your time.'

'No problem.'

As she stepped outside the door, a family passed with groaning children asking when they were going to see Father Christmas.

Holly smiled at them as they walked by, thinking of the time her brother told her that Father Christmas was indeed her dad dressed up. She had spent months feeling depressed over it.

'Hello, Holly,' said a voice.

She snapped out of her thoughts and looked up, surprised to hear her name being called. She looked around and spotted Sue from the hotel loading groceries into the boot of her car.

'Hi, you've been busy, I see?' she asked stopping by the kerb.

'No more than usual, love. So how do you like our little town then? Taken in the sights?'

'It's lovely, reminds me of a Christmas card. Actually, I'm on my way to visit the Christmas tree farm.'

'Thinking of buying a tree for home?'

Holly shook her head. She hadn't hung her stocking in years, and she wasn't about to now.

'No, I'd like to take a look while I'm here.'

'Oh come on, I'll drop you off on my way.'

'Sure?'

'Of course, hop in.'

Sue saw how grateful Holly was for the warmth of the car and chuckled. 'You're not used to our weather, are you?'

Rubbing her hands together, Holly shook her head. 'No, I've never felt anything like it. So, about the farm, what are they doing to raise money?'

'You've heard?' she asked, pulling out.

'I saw it in the shop window.'

'Ah. Well, it's not looking good, I'm afraid. We have a Christmas Ball this Saturday which will hopefully bring in a few quid...are you coming?'

'I'm invited?'

'Of course you are.'

'But I'm only booked until Wednesday.'

'If you change your mind, we'd like to have you.'

'I'll think about it, thanks.'

'Yes, please do, it's going to be spectacular, even if I do say so myself.'

'I'll buy a ticket anyhow, anything to help.'

Susie pulled up outside the entrance to the farm, a wrought iron gate with a snowy path leading to a wooden shed and the forest nestled in the backdrop.

Holly stepped out of the warmth of the car, her shoulders now shaking from the cold. 'Thanks for the lift, Susie.'

'Not a problem, hope you enjoy.'

The yard was busy with customers. She walked past a man and his kids loading a tree onto the roof of his car and strolled on through towards the cabin. With the amount of people buying trees, Holly couldn't understand why they didn't have the means to keep it from closure.

'Can I help you?' asked a man standing by the cabin door with a mug of something warm. He was tall, thin with dark hair greying at the sides.

'I'm just browsing, thanks. Nice place, very Christmassy.'

'Yeah, it's not so bad,' he replied, sadly. 'Unfortunately, I could be closing so it's best if you go to look around now while you've got the chance.'

'Oh?' she realised that he was the owner and now was her chance to introduce herself.

'You're from out of town, are you?'

'Yeah, I'm just here on a shopping trip.'

'Oh well, you wouldn't know then, it's no bother. It's just that I've run this place for over twenty-five years, the last one with my son.'

Holly felt she was intruding but the thought of writing the agony aunt page for another year filled her dread. If she wasn't careful, she'd be writing into the page herself. No, she had to do this.

'May I introduce myself again, I'm Holly Green and I'm a journalist. I think you have an interesting story here; would you be willing to tell it?'

For a brief moment she thought she blew her chances and expected someone to come and march her off the property, but then she saw a glimmer of hope in the man's eyes and let out a little sigh of relief.

'You're from a newspaper?' he asked accusingly.

Holly gulped, thinking she may have read him wrong.

'Yes, I'm from The World, are you familiar with us?'

'I am but more of a sports person myself, so, how do you propose to do this, how will it help us do you think?'

This time she took a deeper breath.

'Well, the paper will highlight your plight and of course I will have to speak to my boss if there is some kind of financial reward, but more importantly, it'll raise awareness of the farm and the village so everyone will benefit in the long run.'

He removed a cigarette from a pack and put it between his lips. 'Alright, I'll talk to you. Meet me at Betty's Diner on the corner of Whistle Street, say, in another hour?'

Hardly believing how easy it was, Holly agreed and put a reminder in her phone. 'I'll see you later then, Mr. Wilson.' She shook his hand.

'Now if you're taking a look around, may I suggest you follow that path,' he pointed, 'it will take you to the highest point and there you'll see for miles. It's the most beautiful view you will ever see.'

'I'll do that and thank you.'

'Enjoy and I'll see you tomorrow.'

She shook his hand once more and set off on the path he suggested. Thinking she ought to take some pictures, she got out her mobile but texted Emily first.

It's in the bag, can't believe how it easy it's been.

The trek up the hill was strenuous, especially with the snow thick under her feet. She stopped to glance back, to see how far she had walked but after all her effort; she saw that she hadn't got far.

Bugger this, she thought and began to make her way back down. A coffee was much needed than looking at a bloody tree. She decided to take one more picture, a selfie with the most gorgeous snowy backdrop, when she saw a reminder on her phone she hadn't checked. It simply said, "Dan." Holly instantly knew what it meant and felt choked. Tears ran down her cool cheeks as she flipped through photos of them together when he was home for the last time. Her thoughts went back to the day she heard he'd passed and quietly sobbed into her scarf.

'It's been a year today. I miss you, babe,' she whispered, leaning against a tree. It took her a few minutes, but she pulled herself together enough to focus on getting back to town and the job at hand.

Looking at all the trees that surrounded her she wondered how special a tree could be that it would become something of a legend, but she wasn't in the mood to find out today. It was icy cold and she had more important things to get on with.

The town was as busy as ever, and not quite ready to go back to the hotel yet, she saw the café she went in earlier and made her way across the road.

She pushed open the glass door to the sound of Elvis Presley's White Christmas, gawping at the waitresses in red uniform dancing behind the counter. Holly smiled, looking around at the customers who whooping and cheering them along. What had she entered into? Standing awkwardly at the door, and determined she wouldn't start swaying her hips also, the song finally ended to a rapturous applause. She closed the door and clapped as she walked towards the counter to place her order.

An older woman with auburn hair and heavy eye make-up came forward. Holly looked around wondering where Betty had got to.

'Hi, hon,' she said breathlessly. A glisten of sweat slicked her forehead. 'Oh excuse me, I'm not young anymore. Would you like a menu or are you ready to order?'

Holly glanced up at the board. 'A burger and side of chips with a cup of tea, thanks.'

While she wrote down the order on a pad, she looked up at Holly. 'Here on holiday or just passing through?' she asked.

'I'm here for a short break, mainly for work,' she took her purse out of her bag. 'I liked your dancing, is this something you normally do?'

The woman laughed. 'From time to time, you know, when the mood takes us. We like to keep it fun and lighthearted here. So, what line of work are you in?'

About to answer Betty came through the kitchen door.

'Holly. How nice of you to come back. How has your day been?'

'Great. I've managed to get Harry's permission to write the article.'

'Wonderful.' Betty turned to the other waitress standing to her side. 'This is the journalist I was telling you about. She's going to write about Harry's plight with the farm.'

'Oh, that's right, I remember you saying now. It's nice to make your acquaintance, Holly.'

Holly took a seat on the high-rise stool when a younger waitress with dark hair came up to the counter.

'There's the delectable Ben, wonder if he's coming in for his regular,' she said to Betty.

'You and that man,' she tutted and flung her tea towel over her shoulder.

Holly's face flushed hot and she unwound her chunky scarf.

'Hot in here isn't?' Betty commented as she handed over a plate of food.

'Gosh yeah,' she glanced out the window just as Ben went inside the bakery opposite.

Chewing on her burger she took her notepad and pen from her bag and set them on the counter, thinking she'd make a start on her article. She took another bite out of her burger but kept being distracted by the waitress's comments about how sexy Ben was and that he must be gay as they'd never seen him with a girl. Holly almost choked on her chip at the hilarious comment. She'd only been here less than a day, and there was no way Ben was gay.

'What are you writing about?' asked the young waitress, topping up her coffee cup and then wiping down the counter with a rag smelling of lemon.

'It's an article about the tree farm. I'm a journalist, or, trying to be. It's my first big job so I need to get this right.'

'You're writing about the farm, eh? Oh, maybe it'll help stop its closure.'

'I'm hoping so.' Surprised by her reaction, Holly put down her pen. 'You think it'll do some good?'

Betty butted in.

'I do, so do what you're good at because this town is nothing without the farm as I have already told you.'

'Thanks for the vote of confidence.'

Armed with motivation and feeling her spirits uplifted, she took her meal to the table beside the window and began scribbling away in her notebook.

Her mobile pinging with a notification took her out of her bubble and, realising she'd been sat for nearly an hour, she looked towards the door hoping Harry would soon be arriving for his interview. The hour passed and there was no sign of Harry. Holly decided to call it a day and packed up her things.

'You're off?' asked Betty handing her the change.

'Rather sadly. Harry didn't turn up like he promised so I think I may have to have a re-think on the whole story.'

'I'm sure he has his reasons, so don't give up just yet, will you? You and this article may just be our saving grace.'

'Thanks for being my number one supporter. I'll keep it in mind.'

Disappointed with the start she had made, she thanked Betty for her coffee refills and left the café, wondering if she was really cut out for this type of work. She walked across the icy pavement to the kerb, overhearing a passing couple talking about a heavy snowstorm that was headed their way this evening. Tucking her scarf tightly into her coat, she thought about going home early. While she waited for the traffic lights to turn green, she checked her phone to see if he had rung or left a message, but there was nothing. As she made her way up the street, she realised she still didn't have her car and that her only option was to walk to her cabin.

'Do you need a lift?' shouted Harry from his car. 'I can drive you to the cabins if you want, it's no problem.'

Delighted she didn't have to trek any more hills, she agreed and got into the passenger side.

'I'm sorry for not turning up, I had a few difficult customers not long after you left and I've only now managed to sort it out. Are you still up for the interview?'

'Of course I am, let's do it now.'

Chapter Nine

'Did you have a good afternoon?'

Holly glanced up from her snow-covered feet to see Clive the owner shovelling snow from his drive.

'It was great, thanks, but still no car.'

'The Mrs has been worried about you.'

'Oh?'

'There's a snowstorm coming, and I don't think it's wise to make your way home tonight.'

Gutted, Holly had to agree. The road down the village was treacherous without the snow.

'Is it okay if I stay another night?'

'Of course, go inside, Susan has made her speciality, hot chocolate.'

'Great, thanks. Sure you don't want any help?'

'No, Ben is supposed to come and help but the bugger hasn't turned up yet.' There was a hint of a laugh in his voice.

She shook her coat of the excess snow flurries and, smelling the aroma of hot chocolate she made her way to the kitchen.

'Hello,' she called out, walking across the foyer to the kitchen at the back of the cabin. The door was open ajar, so she pushed it to find Susan covered in flour, kneading dough.

She looked up, fluttering the dust from her lashes.

'Oh there you are, love. I've been worried.' She wiped her hands with a cloth and gestured to the pot on the stove. 'Would you like some?'

Holly nodded, not feeling her usual self after the moment at the farm. Susie picked up on this.

'Is everything alright? Not worried about the storm, are you? I've been through many here and look...I'm still here.'

'Well, I wish it was just the storm I was worried about,' she pulled out a chair. 'There's a bunch of other things in the mix, personal things, but I'll be fine.'

Susan handed her a large mug of hot chocolate topped with whipped cream. 'Hope you're not counting the calories,' she smiled placing it on the counter in front of her. 'Is there anything I can help with, I'm a good listener, you know.'

'I don't want to burden anyone with my troubles...'

'Don't talk nonsense. Let me pull out a chair, I could do with a break. These,' she pointed to the racks of fairy cakes, 'are for the cake stall tomorrow, but please, have one...'

'Thanks,' she reached out, picking a pink iced cookie instead. 'Well, before I left to come here, my mother gave me an early, or depending on how you look it, a late Christmas present from my fiancé.'

'You're engaged? You never said.'

'I was. He was a soldier...what I mean to say is, he was killed on active duty.'

Susan put a comforting hand on Holly's shoulder. 'I am so sorry darling.'

Holly shrugged, determined not to cry. 'He gave me this,' she pulled out her necklace. Mum forgot to give it to me after everything that had happened. So it sort of spun me out when she gave me it on Saturday.'

'I can imagine, but in some small way, he's still with you, and that necklace is something to treasure. Don't be sad, you should celebrate his life and all that he's achieved. He's a hero.'

'I know, but it was such a surprise.' She took a bite out of her cookie, the soft, warm buttery taste bursting in her mouth. 'These are lovely; I may have to buy a batch to take home with me.'

'Talking of home, did Stan fix your car?'

'In all the kerfuffle today, I forgot about my car,' she laughed.

'There you are, you're laughing already.'

'Thanks for the talk, Susan; I really appreciate you allowing me to get it off my chest.'

'No problem, so are you coming to the light switch on and the ball this Saturday? Oh, plus we have a Christmas market stall in the morning, if this storm buggers off before then.'

Holly sat and thought for a moment, her gaze panning towards the wide; curtain-less windows.

'Yeah, why not, I'll stay another couple of days.'

'There you are then. I say, in a few days maybe even in another week, you'll be back to your old self. These feelings have only been brought to the surface again by the shock of the gift.'

'Yes, I think you're right...'

'Good, so what was the other thing?'

'Oh,' she waved her hand. 'No worries.'

'Sure?'

'I'm writing an article about the Christmas tree farm and I can't help thinking there's more to the selling of the place than what the owner is telling me. I mean, how do you go from owning a property to finding out you owe thousands?'

'You're not the only one to think that. Ben doesn't even know either, but he's supposed to be moving away soon.'

'What's it got to do with Ben?'

'Didn't you know? It's Ben's father that owns it.'

From her room, Holly could see for miles and began to like the idea of staying a few more days. At least she didn't have to get up early for work.

Her phone pinged.

'Hi, Holly, although it's a good piece, I think it needs an emotional, satisfying ending. Please could you get it to me by the end of next week?'

Holly groaned, typing back that she'd get it to her before then, but at the moment she was stuck in the village because of a snowstorm. Expecting a demanding mail to return to work, she was taken aback when Miss Walker replied that it was fine as her article needed her to stay longer.

Sitting at her desk, she took her laptop out of her bag and then leaned back against the seat. About to switch it on, a murmur of conversation could be heard from outside. She stood up and saw Ben and Clive laughing as they loaded a van with boxes.

She grabbed her coat and rushed out of the door, hoping to catch him for a chat about the farm, but just as she got outside, he pulled off and was heading towards the gate. She tried to flag him down, but it was fruitless.

'Everything alright?' asked Clive.

'Yeah, I just wanted to talk to Ben about the farm. I didn't realise it was his dad that owned it.'

'Ah, Susie did tell me you're writing an article on it.' He looked up at the darkening sky. 'I would drive you to the homeless shelter to speak with him, but it's in the next town and the weather looks like it's turning for the worse.'

'Is that where he's going?'

'Yes, every once in a while; Susan makes a batch of goodies to send over. I would've taken it but seeing as Ben was a driver in the army, he said he'd take it, especially with this storm.'

Holly was taken aback by the mention of the army.

'Oh right. So, when do you think he'd be back?'

'Not sure, love. I'd give you his mobile number if I had my phone on me. Ask Susie if she can help you out.'

'Okay, thanks.' She turned back. 'How bad is this storm likely to be?'

'Bad. By tomorrow, everything will be white, mark my words.'

'If it's not so already,' she laughed.

'What you see out there is nothing.'

Chapter Ten

Sat by the window with her laptop resting on the ledge, Holly lifted her head to reflect on the story she had so far. The ending worried her, as she knew there was a risk it wouldn't be a happy one. Figuring she'd written all she could for the evening, she closed down her laptop knowing she couldn't give up on the story yet. If the worst happened, and the story didn't end as their past tear-jerkers had, she was prepared to face her boss and the consequences.

Outside, a wind had whipped up, now rattling the windows. A light still shone from the main cabin indicating that someone was awake. After spending a year living on her own, she wasn't afraid of much, but this evening she desired company so got up to switch on the lamp to find it kept dimming. If the power was going to cut out, she thought could do with a hot chocolate first. Remembering Susan's offer of a chat and beverage earlier that morning, she grabbed her coat from the back of the door noting the time on the bedside alarm clock. It was almost midnight.

She opened the door and saw thick, heavy snowfall, obscuring any view of the village. Beating her way through the bitter cold wind, she saw Susan and Clive in their kitchen window who were waving for her to come inside.

She rapped at the door and within seconds she heard the key rattle and the door swung open.

'Is that you, Holly?' asked Susan, now popping her head round the frame of the door.

'Yes, can't sleep. Sorry if it's late.'

'Oh don't worry, we're night owls ourselves. Come and have a cocoa with us if you want.'

Walking into the kitchen, she was surprised to see the back of Ben reaching in the top cupboard, his tight shirt defining his muscles. Holly averted her eyes to the kitchen counter that was full of freshly baked cookies.

'Hi, Holly, going for an early morning stroll; huh?'

'Hello again, sorry I didn't see you there when I first came in,' she lied.

Embarrassed that she had her dressing gown on under her coat, she tightened the belt as much as she could and sat down on the stool by the island.

'Here you are love,' Susan put a large, red mug down in front of her topped with whipped cream and a sprinkling of cocoa.

'Oh that looks delicious, thank you.'

Clive called Susan from the living room.

'I won't be a minute. Help yourselves to anything to eat.'

Ben picked up his cup of coffee and joined her at the island.

'My van broke down five minutes away from here, so Susan said I could stay the night. So how are you?'

'Good. I was meant to go home today.'

'Yeah, I heard.'

She saw him looking at her dressing gown.

'It's warm,' she replied. 'And no it's not thermal but I wished it was.'

'I think I owe you an explanation.'

'Oh?'

'Yes, it's about the farm. I think you know by now my dad owns it.'

'I do, yeah. I'm sorry to hear you might have to give it up, so are you okay with me writing the article. I remember you saying people didn't want their dirty laundry aired...'

'Sorry, forget I said that. I was being rude, and I only said it because I was afraid you'd find out about the farm.'

'You don't mind me writing then?'

'No. I was talking to Susie about it just now and I agree it may be worth a shot for my old man's sake.'

'Why can't you take the farm on?'

'I don't have the cash to help pay for the leasehold, never mind buying my dad out completely.'

'And who are the party that's interested...'

'I'm not exactly sure. Not long after dad heard the news that the time limit was up for and I quote, "renewing" the leasehold, a guy showed up at the farm expressing an interest in buying it.'

'Coincidence, do you think?'

'That's what I'm wondering. Apparently, his firm builds houses and shopping centres. I don't know if that's what he has planned for it, should he buy it but dad assumes he'll let him rent the farm off of him.'

'It doesn't sound right to me. Call it female intuition or whatever, but something doesn't add up. There has to be a way to get the money to pay the lease.'

'Believe me I've tried. Did you know the farm has been in my family a hundred years this year?'

'Really? And I can't imagine how much of a blow it will be for the town. I was told that it's the heartbeat of the place, right?'

'It truly is. Anyway, I've taken enough of your time already. You must want to get back to bed.'

She looked out the window to gage what time it was, but it was still pitch black.

'It's just gone one o' clock if you're wondering.'

'I suppose I'd better get a few more hours of beauty sleep...'

'It's not like you need it.'

'Oh I do,' she smiled and headed to the kitchen door. About to leave, she stepped back into the kitchen. 'Perhaps we can talk more about this tomorrow?'

'Of course, love to.'

BY THE MORNING, THE storm had gone and the weak, winter sunshine tried to break from the clouds. She locked up the cabin and made her way across the compound to sound of the snow plough on the road. The drive into the place had been cleared and business seemed as though it was back to normal.

'They don't mess about here,' said Clive walking out of the office door, cup of coffee in hand.

'I can see that, so what about the main road out of here. Is that fine?'

He shook his head.

'A load of trees came down, blocking the road. I reckon it'll take another day or so to shift. But if you need to pop into town, it should be fine but best not to walk.'

'Thanks. I may do. I need to see if my car has been fixed.'

'Before you go out in this, why don't you go to the main restaurant? Susie is serving breakfast for everyone in there. You're more than welcome to join her? I'll catch you later, got some calls to make,' he said.

'Okay.'

Christmas music played in the dining room that was empty. She took a seat beside the window and picked up the menu.

'Morning,' said Susan popping up from behind the bar. 'I'm just doing a stock take. Do you want to order a breakfast, I'm about to cook more anyway?'

'I'd love a cooked breakfast thanks, I'm starved.'

'Oh, before I forget,' she fished in her apron pocket. 'Ben left this for you this morning,' she handed her a piece of paper. 'He said if you'd like to meet him later, he'll be at the café.'

'Thanks.' She set the note aside and scanned through the menu once more. 'I'll have scrambled eggs on toast and a black tea.'

'It's coming right up.'

Once Susan went into the kitchen, she snatched up the note and unfolded it excitedly. It was like school all over again. 'Oh no,' she muttered. Was she developing feelings for him?

'Hey Holly, meet me at the café around 1pm.'

Ben x

She exhaled, read the note again and tucked it into her mobile case reminding herself that it wasn't a date.

After breakfast she said goodbye to Susan, thinking she'd try to walk into town, giving her a chance to mull over the story she had to write. She had a good feeling about the story, and that it had plenty of potential – if only she could find it. Clive called after her as she made her way to the main gates.

'Need a lift?' he asked.

'If you don't mind,' she shivered.

'You'll need to get some thermals,' said Clive, now laughing. 'Go to The Mill, you won't regret it.'

Remembering her bet with Ben, The Mill was the last place she wanted to be seen.

'Thanks, I'll keep it in mind.'

Conveniently, Clive dropped her off outside The Mill. She thanked him for the lift and got out, wondering if she should invest in something that would stop the cold reaching her bones.

She waved goodbye to Clive and then looked around the busy street, feeling a little stupid. Nobody knew her here, and after all it was only a silly bet, so surely he won't hold her to it. She sucked in a cold, sharp breath and then walked into the shop. The door pinged and a man walked out of the storeroom to greet her.

'Hello, can I help you or do you wish to browse first?' he asked.

Holly glanced around the shop that also sold ski gear and sleds. 'Well, I was wondering if you sold...'

'Thermals?' he said, cheekily. 'We get a lot of tourists in here buying the stuff, so you won't be the first.' He came around the counter and went to a shelf next to a mannequin dressed as Santa Claus in a skiing suit.

'Here we are,' he handed her a few items to look at. 'These are new in. If you need any more help, let me know.'

'Thank you,' she exhaled when he back to the counter. She sifted through the clothing, selecting a long sleeve, black top and took it to the counter.

'Would you mind if I pay for this now and then use your changing room to put it on?' she asked, opening her purse.

'Of course you may, not a problem. So are you here for the Winterfest?' He asked, scanning the tag.

'Um, I may not actually stay for the weekend,' she replied, remembering it was Ben's friend she was speaking to. She handed him the correct cash, said thank you, and headed to the changing room before making a quick exit out of there.

She pulled open the diner's doors to the loud Christmas music, glad of the warmth hitting her cold cheeks.

'You're back, how's the story going?' asked Betty, holding up two trays with burgers and fries as she sashayed around tables.

'I couldn't get home what with the snow, but the story is going well. Lot's more to do, so could I have a coffee? I'll be over there,' she pointed to a booth at the far end of the room.

'No problem, love. I'll bring it over.'

Walking past the counter the two younger waitresses were leaning on the bar deep in conversation.

'So do you think you should ask him to the Winterfest ball, then?'

'Who are you talking about?' The other woman replied.

'Ben. Who do you think I was talking about?'

Holly's ears pricked at the mention of Ben's name and gave them her full attention as she sat down in her favourite spot. She had to admit, he was a good looking guy, so it was no wonder he had the local female population talking.

She pulled out her laptop from her bag and placed it on the table.

'There's free WIFI,' said Betty, placing down her coffee and a large slice of chocolate gateau. 'Despite what people may think, we do keep up with the modern world.'

'Oh that's great, thanks. And wow, I must be becoming a regular for you to know my order before I ask.' She indicated to the cake.

'It's my special talent. After thirty years in the business, you can almost sense what people want before they ask for it.'

'Can you really?'

'No, I'm kidding, love. I've just made this and you're my guinea pig. It's on the house.'

'Oh thank you.'

'I don't know if you've already found this out, but have you heard of the legend surrounding that farm?'

Intrigued, Holly gestured her to sit down. 'No, I haven't, and if you're not busy, I'd like to hear it.'

Betty shouted to the girls at the bar to get on with their work.

'I'm due a break,' she said, then ordering one of the girls to fetch her over a coffee.

Betty sighed as she sat down. 'I'm glad to take the weight off my feet. So where was I? Oh yes,' she wagged a finger, 'The legend of the Christmas tree farm.'

'Sounds exciting,' said Holly, hugging her warm cup.

'Well it is and it isn't, depending on who's telling the story. There's a darker side to the legend that used to keep me awake at nights when I was a child. You see, my father used to tell me there was a ghost hanging around the tree farm and that if all the children in the village didn't behave, he'd tell Father Christmas not to fetch us presents. Of course, I later learned this wasn't the truth,' she chuckled.

Holly loved stories; she even started writing a novel once but gave up when she couldn't decide on an ending for it. She made a mental note to get back to it one day.

'So what happened,' she answered eagerly.

'I suppose you've heard about the special tree on the top of the hill?'

'Oh yes; the famous Christmas tree.'

'Well that was supposedly given to the town many years ago by a passing stranger. Some say he was an old man; some say he was a ghost but anyway, he was lost out there on the mountains when Ben's four times great grandfather found him and helped him find his way. In return he gave him a twig and told him to plant it in the ground so that one day it'll grow to be prosperous and bring him riches, but he must never ever sell it.'

'Is this really true?'

'Nobody quite knows for sure, not even Ben's dad. It's why they have never sold the tree or the farm. When a family member retires, another must take over, no outsiders.'

'So why haven't it brought him luck now?'

'Ever since Ben has said he's moving; Ben's dad has had rotten luck. He asked Ben to take over but Ben has other plans and to be quite honest with you, since then it hasn't felt like Christmas around here. It feels like the magic is going.'

'I wonder.'

'What do you wonder?'

Holly couldn't believe she was thinking it as she was quite a rational person, but ever since she heard Betty tell her the tale, she kept thinking of the way her own life had spiralled since losing her fiancé.

'I wonder if his lack of love for the season has caused this to happen.'

'That's one speculation. Though it doesn't help that Ben has had a job offer in Canada.'

'He's moving? That's a shame.'

'Talk of the devil, here he comes,' she said, getting up from her seat.

Holly looked over her shoulder just as Ben pushed open the door. The girls were giggly behind the counter when he approached them.

The flirtation was so bad, Holly snorted with laughter and returned to her coffee; taking her pen and jotting down notes of the story she had been told.

'Hey, it's nice to see you, Holly.'

She twisted in her seat, acting surprised to see him.

'You got my note then?'

'Yes, of course. Thanks for being here, take a seat.'

'He shrugged his shoulders. 'It's alright. I know how much this article means to you.'

'Yeah, it does actually mean a lot to me. So... busy day at work?'

'Come on, Holly, you're not interested in my day. You need to get this article written, so shall we?'

'Of course,' she lied, thinking how she would've liked to have heard how his day was, but thought it was best to keep things on a professional level, and not confuse his friendship with anything else. The man needed her help; besides she knew that if Emily was here, she'd say she was falling for him. She shrugged off the ridiculous thoughts.

Holly began to tell him the story she heard from Betty.

'That's sort of the story, yes, but that old story isn't going to help keep the farm. These guys in suits don't care about anything but money.'

'What's happened?'

'Last night, dad agreed to sell it on. I think he's given up. The solicitor says there's nothing he can do about the sale if we can't come up with the cash on Christmas Eve. According to him it's all legit – we're going to lose our livelihoods and there's nothing anyone can do about it. But Holly, that's not the worst thing. The people who are interested in the place have duped my dad into thinking they'd buy it out to keep the farm going, but I've heard from reliable sources they're planning something far worse.'

'Do the people of the town know?'

'Not exactly, but let's say secrets don't stay secrets here for long. Besides, I don't know how to tell them.' He whispered. 'Look, let's get out of here,' he gave a nod towards the counter, at the two waitresses checking them out. 'Prying eyes and ears...'

Holly nodded and got her coat from the back of her chair. Ben went to pay his bill, taking his wallet out of the back pocket of his denims.

'I've paid yours, too,' he held up a receipt.

'You didn't have to,' she said, slipping her bag over her shoulder.

'Well, let's say you owe me one,' he grinned. 'I've just had a message from my old pal at The Mill. Someone of your description just bought a thermal top.' He winked.

Holly pursed her lips; sure, she'd got away with it. The two girls at the counter were now watching her with keen interest.

'Okay, dinner it is.'

'Plus dessert, don't forget.'

'How could I forget,' she shrugged, smiling at the girls as she passed. The hateful look on their faces was the best thing she'd seen all day.

'Oh Holly, by the way, I was joking about the thermals. It's an inside joke the townsfolk have, I'm sorry.'

'Nice one. I've just spent twenty-five pounds on a top, but actually, it's quite comfortable and warm so I'm not really complaining.'

Chapter Eleven

Ben stepped in front of her and held open the door. 'After you.'

'Thanks.' She stepped out of the café, wondering if she really had to keep her bet, but then, it wasn't as though he was hinting at a date with her, right? It was just a couple of drinks and food. It'll be her way of saying thanks for the help with her car.

'So, where are we going for dinner?'

Holly stood on the busy pavement; her mouth gaped open, trying to decipher if he was joking with her or not. He smiled widely, almost teasing, or was he? She still wasn't sure. Ben raised an eyebrow awaiting a response from her, but she still couldn't gage if he was about to burst out laughing should she agree. She'd been out of the dating game since she met Dan at eighteen and now wished she'd paid more attention to Emily on their nights out.

'Oh you actually mean it?'

'Of course I do, a bet is a bet. Hey, I'll pay half, is that a fair deal?'

Being a soft touch, she gave in. 'Sure, you can pick when.'

'Well, how about tomorrow? Are you doing anything?'

She shrugged. 'I was thinking about washing my hair.'

'You are?'

'No, it was a joke. I'm not doing anything important tomorrow that I know of, so yeah alright I'll pay the other half.'

Ben became distracted by something behind her. Holly looked over her shoulder, but all she could see were crowds of people having a good time.

'What's wrong?' she asked.

'I can't believe what I'm seeing. Holly, you'd better come with me and I'll explain.' He took her hand and began running down the street.

'What did you see?' Holly asked, trying her hardest to keep up pace with Ben.

When they got to street corner, at the zebra crossing, he stopped abruptly as a car came around the corner. She saw him sneer at the blacked-out windows.

'I'm sorry, Holly. I know you must think I'm a mad man, but I'll explain in a minute.' Without warning, he ushered her across the road.

'Woah, can we slow down now?' she asked, trying to catch her breath.

'Yeah, you see; the guy that's interested in the farm passed in that car just now. with my solicitor. I don't know what the hell is going on,' he said angrily, but I'm going to find out.'

'Who's your solicitor, maybe my dad can help.'

'Harold Murphy. I always thought he was a two-faced git, but he and my dad go way back so I don't say anything. Anyway, I wonder if you'd like to come to my place for a coffee or something, until I can figure out what to do.'

'Is it far?'

'No, just on that mountain there,' he pointed with a grin.

Holly knew he was joking with her. 'That's a shame, I can't walk up there. I don't have any snow grips on my boots.'

'That's why I have a car. Come on, I'm parked outside the bakery.'

'You parked a long way from the diner. Afraid to be seen with me?' she jostled, as they walked up the street.

Ben scoffed and opened the door for her. 'Are you kidding? No, I had a feeling I was being followed the night I met you.'

She got in the car, wondering what was happening.

'Do you mean the guys who are interested in the farm have been following you?'

'Yes,' he put on his seatbelt.

'Why would they do that?'

'I think they know I'm talking to you; that's why.'

'They know I'm a journalist. And that's a bad thing?'

'There's millions at stake here for them, so of course they're on their toes.'

'Crap. So they could potentially stop my story?'

'That might be their intention, but the most they'll do is to try to scare you off.'

'But who could've told them I'm here?'

'It's a small town, Holly. One time, when I was a kid, dad took me the dentist, and everyone knew I was having a tooth out before I did. If I knew what I was getting into I would've bolted when I had the chance.'

Holly laughed hard.

'There, you don't seem so worried now,' he touched her lightly on the arm.

She gave him a tight-lipped smile in return, feeling awkward.

'Yeah, so, where do you live?'

'Just... here.' He pulled up on the drive of a thatched roof cottage just outside the town.

'I saw these when we were coming into the village, they're so pretty they should be on postcards.'

'They already are.' He unclipped his belt and got out of the car. 'You can buy some from Cooper's Newsagents.'

Holly grabbed her bag and opened the door.

'Watch the ice,' he said, rushing around the car to her aid. He held out a hand, grabbing hers just as she felt the ice slick beneath her feet.

'Thanks.' She held on to his coat, pulling herself up from an embarrassing position.

'Don't mention it.' He tucked his arm in hers and walked her across the black ice to his front door.

Once the door opened, Holly was confronted by a barrage of boxes stacked in the hallway.

'Ah, I've been packing, so forgive the mess.'

'I did hear you're moving. Where to?' she asked, taking a large step over a box.

'Well, dad is convinced the farm is going, so there's nothing left for me here. I'm going to work in Canada.'

'What if your dad wasn't considering selling, do you think you'd stay?'

'Then I'd probably had taken over the farm and no, I can't help out dad with money. I've nothing since coming back from the army. This place is rented and pretty cheap since the guy who owns it is my cousin.'

'I can see why it's cheap,' she shivered. 'Is there any heating here?'

'I'll chuck some logs on the fire. Do want to give me a hand to get the logs?'

'Sure. It's not like I have a story to write or anything,' she joked.

Ben laughed. 'It could be worse, you could be stuck in an office all day, but no,' he pushed open his front door,' you're collecting wood with me in the most beautiful part of the world.'

Holly was a bit reluctant to go outside the door. 'You don't think they'll be hanging around, do you?'

'No, don't worry, I'm here, aren't I?'

'Hark at you. What are you now, my bodyguard? Hang about, wasn't it you who ran away from them just now?' she laughed.

'Funny aren't you.'

'So I've been told.'

Ben walked around the side of the house, to the back garden that backed onto a wooded area.

'Dad's farm starts here,' he pointed over his red painted fence.

'It does? That must be handy when you need to get to work.'

'Yeah, but for how long it's ours, who knows,' he shrugged almost on the verge of tears.

'Hey, come on,' she picked up some logs from the bunker. 'Stop thinking the worse. Anything could happen between now and Christmas Eve.'

Ben crouched down next to her, stacking logs into his arms. 'You're right. It's hard to think of the positives when you've seen what I have...' he shook his head as if to say he didn't want to talk about it further. Holly understood too well. Now would've been the opportune moment to talk about Daniel, yet she still couldn't find it within herself to open up about her past. Why did she have to be so stubborn?

'Oh wow, did you see that?' she jumped to her feet. 'I think I saw a deer by the broken part of the fence. Look,' she whispered, pointing to the farthest end of the garden.

'Isn't he gorgeous,' Ben said, inching closer to her. 'That's the beginning of my dad's woods, care for a walk around? It'll keep us warm.'

'Sure. But let me just text my dad first...'

'Oh? I thought you were old enough to make your own decisions,' he joked.

'Very funny but I was going to text him about the guys who were following you.'

'Honestly, Holly, they won't lay a finger on you, it's not worth their while. But, just to reassure you okay, I'm going to let the local sheriff know what's going on.'

'Okay, great. Just let me take these logs inside first, get a fire going for later.'

'Are you ready for your guided tour?' he asked, pulling up the collars of his coat.

'Sure am,' replied Holly ducking under the broken fence. Ben followed after her, tucking his hands in his pockets. He offered his arm to her as they started walking towards the cluster of snow-covered trees.

'Nice to know chivalry still exists.' She accepted his gesture and linked his arm, surprised how tightly he held her close. For the first time in a long time, she felt protected and secure. She exhaled deeply, allowing her inhibitions about another man touching her in this way dissolve into the ether. The moment seemed right in her mind and that's all that mattered.

As they walked, swaying around the trunks, Ben pointed out the different names of the trees until they came to the cabin where they sold the Christmas trees to the public.

'Have you seen our most famous tree, yet?' he asked with a cheeky glint in his eyes.

'No but I've heard a lot about it.'

'You have? What have you heard?' he asked, heading towards a steep hill.

'Yeah, firstly Betty told me, and your dad confirmed it was a gift to his three times great grandfather.'

'I can't believe he's still harping on about it.'

'Why?'

'Well, I think it was a story to entice people to come here, you know, for the magical Christmas feeling you see on the Hallmark channel...'

'Ah, so you're a non-believer.'

'I didn't say that exactly, but you can't pin your whole life on a wishy washy story, can you?' He replied, catching his breath. 'And here she is,' he pointed to a tall, elegantly looking tree stood on its own, away from the others. Around its base it had a wooden fence with a small sign stating it was the Christmas tree given to the family over two hundred years ago.

Holly stopped for a breather and stepped back to look at the tree. It seemed lonely on its own, but it stood tall and proud; its branches lightly dusted with glittering snow in the waning sunlight. Her whole life revolved around creating stories. Where would she have been without them as a child? Surely, he could understand that.

'Stories are like dreams, Ben. We need them to function in our everyday life…'

'We need oxygen and food to function, not stories.'

'You see everything so black and white, don't you?'

'Well, being in the army, and seeing what I did, it's hard to believe in miracles and what not…' He waved his hand, seemingly not wanting to talk anymore.

Holly dismissed the hint.

'As I was saying, the story around this tree might sound wishy washy to you, but it brought hope to many people. It's like this, Ben. When reality hits you so hard, and believe me I have been hit so hard, writing and stories have pulled me from the black hole I'm in and says, yes, you have to keep believing in a better tomorrow.'

'Why?'

'Because life is beautiful, you just have to adjust your perception of it a little.' At that moment, Holly closed her eyes, realising the advice she had given Ben was exactly what she needed to hear herself. 'For the past year I've been grieving hard. Some days were better than others, but now, today, at this moment, I feel like the old me is creeping back again.'

Ben walked towards her and placed his hands on her shuddering shoulders.

'I do know what you mean, Holly. Since you've been here, my cold, hard exterior is slowly chipping away, too.' He looked deep into her eyes. 'And look, I'm sorry for being so uptight just now. I've always tried to be the strong one for everyone and I admit; I've been lost too. It's time to start believing in life again, right?'

Through tear-stained eyes, Holly nodded and leaned in for a hug, immersing herself in Ben's strong arms now wrapped around her. A few moments passed by before they broke from the embrace; looking at each other. Ben moved in slowly, tilting her chin with his finger. Holly closed her eyes feeling his hot breath closing in on hers. Gently, he pressed a kiss on her lips and Holly responded back, surprised at herself. Maybe she had healed more than she had thought. She pulled back, slightly embarrassed and looked down at her feet.

'Hey,' Ben said softly, caressing her cheek. 'There's nothing to worry about, it was totally fine with me.'

Holly met his eyes. 'I guess that's okay, then. So, come on, show me the rest of the place, although what else is there to see in a wood? If you've seen one tree you've seen them all.'

Ben smiled, wagging a finger at her. 'Not necessarily...'

'Oh?'

'There's about a dozen different types of trees here...'

'So what's that one?' She pointed to the Christmas tree.

'A spruce.'

'Oh, says the man who doesn't want anything to do with the farm, you seem to know an awful lot.'

'I had no choice. I only started helping out, so I'd have pocket money to buy the latest Transformer figures.'

Holly followed his lead; her thoughts consumed by their kiss.

When they arrived back at the house, Holly's phone pinged with notifications.

'Ah, looks like we're back in the land of the living,' Ben said, stepping into his house. He gestured Holly inside, but she held up her hand.

'Just a moment, I need to ring my cousin back,' she replied with the phone against her ear.

'Hey, Holly,' said Sarah. 'Emily told me what's happening, are you alright?'

Holly wasn't surprised to hear this as Sarah's parents lived in the same area as Emily's and were always visiting each other.

'Yes, of course I am. How's dad...'

'Your dad is bloody furious and asked me to ring you to let you know he's looking into the company as we speak...'

'But dad is retired. I really shouldn't have bothered him with this.'

'Your dad still has friends at the police station. If he finds out anything, I'll let you know. Now are you sure you don't want to forget the whole thing and come home?'

'No, are you bloody joking. I've got an article to write. It's my only chance to prove to Walker I am just as capable as anyone.'

'Well you'd better keep that hunk beside you...'

'How do you know about him? Oh let me guess, Emily, right? Does she tell you everything?'

'Pretty much,' she laughed. 'I don't mean to sound insensitive, but have you thought of dating again? It's been a long time, Holly.'

'Look, I know you mean well, but I really don't want this discussion now...I'll speak to you soon.'

'Is it because he's there with you now?'

Holly rolled her eyes. 'I'm going now, Sarah. Let me know what dad finds out.'

She exhaled deeply, got off the phone and went inside the house; happy to feel the warmth on her face from the fire.

'Hey, I'm in the kitchen,' yelled Ben. 'Do you want tea or coffee?' He asked, pointing to the machine. 'I have the fancy stuff, or we can go all out and have the granules.'

'Let's have the fancy stuff since you're offering.' She pulled out a chair and sat down. 'So, there's no wife or girlfriend...boyfriend?'

Ben spat out the biscuit he'd put in his mouth and set the tin down on the table.

'No to all three. I haven't been in a relationship since I got back from duty.' He picked up the percolator, brought it to table and poured hers into a large mug.

Holly couldn't bring herself to talk about Daniel and allowed him to carry on with his story. Ben sat down, his knee almost brushing against hers.

'I lost my best mate, and ... I came home to find my girlfriend had upped and left me. No word, no warning. And ever since then I've been working for dad while I figured out the rest of my life.'

'I'm sorry about your friend,' she said choking back tears. She picked up her cup, trying to get a hold of herself before she poured her heart out to him.

'It's war. Senseless, but no matter how much you prepare for it, it's never enough. Anyway, so tell me about you. Why do you want to be a journalist?'

'I just like stories. In bad times they help you make sense of the world. I still think you ought to fight for the farm you know. There's something wonderful about that place.'

Ben shrugged. 'I'll have a think about it, I promise. I don't know what it is, but I've wanted to break with family tradition and do my own thing for a long time. Now the place is in trouble, and we could lose it, I'm starting to think that maybe, yes, it is what I want.'

'That's just it, isn't it? It's only when we're about to lose something we truly appreciate it. Look, do you have a laptop I could use? I'd like to get something written while I'm here...'

'So you're not going to let them get to you.'

'No. No I'm not. I think this story needs to be told and what you've just said is perfect.'

Chapter Twelve

'I'm glad you're continuing with the story. I can only guess someone must've blabbed without realising it. I'm really sorry,' said Susie pinning a garland on the foyer wall. 'Despite what you may think, there are some horrible buggers in this town that would love to see the farm go under.'

'It's fine, honest. I've already written most of the story. It's just the "emotionally satisfying ending," my editor wants is the hardest part to write.'

'Let it come naturally. Now, could you pass me the mistletoe?' she pointed towards a box on the table brimming with tinsel.

'Sure.'

Holly rummaged in the cardboard box for the mistletoe and thought she saw something dark passing the pane of glass. Startled, she looked up and saw a man in a three quarter length black coat push open the door and stepped into the foyer. He nodded politely at them both and went to the desk.

'Susie, it looks like you've got a customer.' Holly held up the mistletoe.

'Oh, do you mind?' she passed Holly the mistletoe and stepped down from the ladder.

'No, I don't mind at all,' Holly got up the ladder while Susie went to see to the gentleman.

As she pinned the mistletoe in the wall, she couldn't help overhearing their conversation.

'Just the two nights, is it?'

'Yes, hopefully business won't take too long.'

'What sort of business are you in?' she asked, putting his details into the computer.

The man hesitated a moment, which only intrigued Holly more.

'Cars.' He finally answered. 'I import and export cars.'

'Nice, so can I take your name please.'

'Alex Smith.'

Holly scoffed at his name. Couldn't he come up with something more original than Smith?

When Susie gave him his keys, he nodded again at Holly as he passed to the exit.

'I don't trust him,' said Susie, stepping around the counter.

'Me either. Why stall when someone asks you your line of business. It shouldn't be something you have to think about, right?'

'Agreed. From now on you work with me and don't mention anything about newspapers around here. Not until we get to the bottom of this whole thing. Anyway, I'm off to the Winterfest meeting, do you fancy coming along?'

'Winterfest meeting?' she asked, halfway down the ladder.

'We're discussing the parade and sorting out who is doing what float. I can't promise it'll be fun, but there'll be free coffee and cake.'

'I'm sold.'

It was only a short drive to the community hall. Women were being dropped off by their husbands; cheerily waving back at them with a bottle or two in their hands as they drove off.

Holly felt she was in for a wild night, possibly even wilder than her jaunts out with Emily in Soho. Upon entering the community hall, a woman handed her a glass of wine.

'Nice to see you here, love. How's the story going?'

She shouldn't have been surprised to hear that everyone knew what she was doing in Christmas Village but she was.

'It's going well...'

Betty came over. 'Stop harassing the girl, Lil.'

'I'm not, you cheeky...'

'Don't start ladies,' said Susie, stepping between them. 'We've only just arrived and already you're at each other's throats.'

Holly stood in the flyer, listening to them all talking. She thought the place was crazy, but in a good way.

Susie shook her head at Holly. 'Those pair,' she rolled her eyes. 'They're sister in laws. Never liked each other and probably never will.'

The hall itself was decorated with a large tree, and the raised stage was covered in props for the annual Christmas show. When everyone had settled down onto their seats and got down to business, Holly received a message on her phone. She apologised and went outside to answer. Once she got outside, she breathed heavily with relief. Part of her didn't want to go back inside to the craziness. Walking down towards the main road, she heard someone whistling, and then saw Ben walking along the footpath on the opposite side of the road.

'Hey,' she yelled waving.

For a moment it didn't seem he had heard her then his dog began barking.

'Hey, Holly,' he sounded subdued, not like his cheery self she was familiar with.

She stepped of the slush of snow and ran across the empty road, slipping on the ice.

Ben rushed over to her.

'Are you alright?' he asked, his face inches above hers.

'Yeah, I'm fine.' She sat up, rubbing her back. 'I feel like such an idiot.'

Ben laughed, his breath fanning into the inky black sky twinkling with stars. 'You seemed in a rush to see me,' he joked and held out a hand to her.

She accepted his help, and he pulled her to her feet. 'I wouldn't say that I was in a rush but boy was I glad to get out of there.' She thumbed to the community hall.

'The annual "Christmas float meeting"', he said cheekily. 'Yeah, it's the same every year. It's just an excuse for all the women from the village to have a piss-up. I think my dad told me once even the cake is laced with alcohol.'

'They must come out of there steaming by the night is over,' she laughed. 'Talking of your dad, the guy who's supposedly buying the farm is staying at The Cabin. I saw him earlier.'

'Oh,' Ben sighed heavily and started walking down the path again. 'You can follow me if you like,' he turned back at Holly.

'Are you sure I'm not interrupting?'

'Not at all, I'll be glad of the company. Besides, I do it most nights, ever since I got back...'

'Got back?' she asked and then inwardly chastised herself when she realised what he meant.

'When I got back from Afghanistan,' he replied quietly.

'I don't sleep much either.'

'No?' He asked, surprised. He pointed towards a bench, visible by the silvery glow of the moon on the lake.

Holly noticed a single tree in the water, its branches covered with baubles. She pointed at it. 'Nothing is left undecorated here, is it?'

'No, absolutely nothing is left. Shall we sit down? Your back might still be a bit sore...'

'Sure, thanks.' She tucked in her coat and crossed her arms across her chest to keep some semblance of warmth.

'So why don't you sleep, huh? Are you too busy writing and burning and the midnight oil?'

'I wish it was that simple, too. But no, tell me about you, did you retire from the army?'

Ben shook his head. 'No. As I said, I saw my best mate...' He exhaled and rested back against the seat. 'Sorry, I...'

'It's alright,' she said, feeling bad for opening her big mouth. 'I do understand,' she whispered. 'It's gorgeous here...' she said, trying to change the topic of conversation.

'It's beautiful,' he turned to Holly. 'It's such a shame I made plans to leave when all this is over.'

'You don't think you'll stay then?'

'I can't get my hopes up things will work out. Besides, I don't want to stay here either and walk past it as a constant reminder of the good times, you know.'

'Things may turn around, you never know...'

'Holly, I wish I could have an ounce of your optimism, but every day is another day with no way to raise the funds. In fact, I heard last night that our time limit is up. They exchange contracts and whatever on Christmas Eve.

'I've an idea, bear with me alright.'

Intrigued, Ben turned to face her. 'Okay, but I mean this in the nicest possible way. I'm not expecting much, so don't go worrying yourself if you can't fix it.'

'Gosh, you are a pessimist, aren't you?'

'I guess I am. Come on, we'll give you a lift back to your cabin.'

When they arrived at the Gingerbread Cabins, Ben got out of the car and walked Holly to her cabin when he hushed her up. 'Do you hear that?' He pushed her into the shadow and pointed to a man standing outside another cabin talking on the phone.

'Has the building application been approved?' he said. 'I have five big retailers agreeing to this and you say they don't want in?'

'Oh shit,' Ben whispered. 'My dad is going to be devastated.'

Chapter Thirteen

Holly didn't know how she was going to achieve the ending for her story. Christmas was three weeks away and, as she stared at her half-finished first draft, she almost wished she was still writing the agony aunt section. Well, for a brief moment until she had a flashback of being bored at the office.

Checking her emails, she saw a reply from the other journalist and quickly opened it.

Hi, Holly, sorry it took so long to get back to you. I had an emergency caesarean and haven't had the energy to do much. You know what babies are also like, keeps you busy. I was covering the Winterfest and the women who have run it for the past thirty years. Hope this helps.

Felicity x

'Fantastic.' If only she had stuck to her original idea and covered the Winterfest, she wouldn't be stuck with a story that had the potential to turn into something dangerous if she wasn't careful. She sat on her ledge and looked out of the window at the snow flurries.

'What do I do, Dan?' she whispered, pressing her head to the cold glass. A dark shadow passed her line of vison, and she raised her eyes to see a man carrying a Christmas tree across the grounds towards the main cabin. 'I'll take that as a sign then, shall I?' she smiled, assured her decision to cover the tree farm was the correct one. She closed the half-open curtains and got into her fleece onesie.

She awoke the following morning to her phone ringing.

'Hi, mum, what is it?'

'I thought you were coming home yesterday, why didn't you ring? I popped around to your flat but you weren't there.'

'Sorry, I did text dad to say we had a snowstorm, and I couldn't get the car out.'

'Well as long as you're alright. You are alright, aren't you?'

'Yes,' she threw the bedcover off and sat up. 'I have a story I'm chasing, so as soon as this Winterfest weekend is over, I'll be home and we'll go shopping.'

'Shopping for Christmas? Okay, what have you done with my Holly?'

Holly laughed, slipping her feet into her slippers.

'She's still here. I think she got a bit lost for a while.'

'Well, I'm glad to know she's back. Give me a call to say when you're on the way home, okay, love. See you soon.'

'I will do. Bye.' She switched off her phone and slung it across the bed. The fire was almost out and it was freezing. Opening her suitcase, she got out a fresh, clean jumper and jeans and was about to take a shower when she lifted the curtain to see what it was like outside. The snow trickled down, and as she lowered the curtain, she saw the businessman getting into his car on the drive.

'Watch out, I'm onto you,' she whispered before heading into the shower.

SHE MANAGED TO GET a ride with a couple who were staying at the cabins to the tree farm.

'Thanks for the ride, enjoy your day.' She got out of the car, surprised to see Ben and Harry standing outside the gates with the man she saw at the cabins earlier. From the sound of their voices, it didn't look like they were having a pleasant conversation.

'And *her*,' the man pointed to Holly. 'A pathetic sob story in the paper isn't going to save your ass. Face it, you've lost. I don't see why you can't hand the documents over to me now.'

'We still have until Christmas Eve no matter what you say, Mr whoever you are, so get off their property, why don't you, before I call the local sheriff.' She waved her mobile at him.

He scowled. 'Christmas Eve and it's mine.' He took off back to his car parked on the roadside.

'Someone woke up on the wrong side of bed this morning, huh?' she nodded to the guy.

Ben looked pained.

'I'm sorry, Holly. I just told dad what we heard last night. It's only a matter of time before the whole town finds out.'

'So you're preparing for a headache and a barrage of questions from the locals then?'

'Jeez, I don't know what we're going to do.' He ran his hands through his tousled hair. 'If this farm goes, it's going to break this town. It's already breaking my dad.'

'We should call a town meeting, what do you say?'

'And get the blame for all this? I don't know if I can handle it right now.'

'If people knew what was really going on, they will do even more to help. I'll help you set it up.'

'Is this just for your article?'

'No. I care, I really do.'

He sighed. 'Okay, I think it's for the best. Meet me at the café later on?'

'Of course I will. It's not like I can go anywhere without a car, is it?'

The preparations for the Winterfest were already underway when she walked down the high street. As she passed the square, people were busy setting up stalls and beside the Christmas tree a man dressed as Santa Claus had just got off his sleigh with real reindeer and was about to walked into his grotto; a smaller version of the cabins she was staying in.

Betty called out from the shop doorway.

'How's it going?' Holly shouted over the sound of a lorry's engine. The guy fixing the lights on top of the crane also shouted down "hello" to her.

Holly looked up, gave him a wave and then stood by the kerb, looking for any oncoming traffic.

'Come inside a minute,' said Betty.

Curious, Holly went inside, took off her woolly hat that loosened her hair over her shoulders. 'Can I have a cup of tea while I'm here?' She rubbed her hands for warmth.

Betty went around the counter, yelling to a customer that she'd be right over with a menu.

'Did you know about the, you know...' she winked.

Holly leant forward of the counter. 'What are we talking about?' she whispered.

'I heard from Harry that the farm will be turned into a new housing estate and shopping centre.'

Holly straightened up. 'I may have heard something too.'

'Ben's dad called in on his way home last night. The man is in pieces, hell, the town is going to be in uproar when they find out their livelihoods are at stake.'

'Look, we need to arrange a meeting with everyone in town, including the mayor – who is the mayor?' she asked.

Betty put down her mug of tea, smirking. 'It's me.'

'It's you! Really?'

'Yes, seventeen years now. Okay, what I suggest is, if I contact every business owner in the village tonight to arrange to meet them at my house, that way, it'll be our little secret, hm?'

'That's brilliant, thank you. There must be a way to raise this money...'

'A hundred thousand is a lot, to be honest, I don't like our chances.'

Chapter Fourteen

Feeling pleased with herself; Holly walked carefully across the icy cobblestones with a steaming cup of coffee in her hands. Her phone pinged with several messages. She sat down on the bench outside a toy shop and checked her phone.

Hi, Holly, I've had my pals to do a search the firm and they're not to be trusted. They've done a lot of underhanded deals that I'm aware. Apparently, we have several files on them but haven't caught them to bring them to justice.

Dad x

'Got you,' she blurted out loud unaware of a family passing. The youngest child giggled and pointed a finger at her. 'Oh you know,' she waved her phone. 'Candy Crush,' she laughed, thinking she'd better hurry to Ben's place to tell him the news.

When she pulled up at his house, the boot of his car was open, stuffed with boxes. She unclipped her belt, grabbed her phone off the dashboard and got out of the car, dashing to the open front door.

'Ben? Are you home?'

'In here, Holly.'

She wiped her snow slushed boots on the Darth Vader Welcome mat and went into the living room.

Ben was stooped over a box, mid-way to putting in a pile of books.

'I know what this looks like...'

'You're leaving now? But...but you can't.'

He dropped the books to the box and stepped around it, gently placing a hand on Holly's shoulder.

'Dad has almost given up and I have nothing to stay here for,' he said looking longingly at her. 'The guy who is offering me a job wants someone over there now and I'm available,' he shrugged. 'I can leave tomorrow.'

'Can't you wait until after the Winterfest?' she said then remembering why she came. 'Bugger, I forgot, the reason I came here was to tell you that my dad has found out something that may change your mind.'

He motioned her to an empty part of the sofa, but she declined.

'The solicitor, the development firm, they're all in on it. They're ripping you off and apparently, they do it all the time to acquire land.'

Ben's face darkened.

'What?'

'There may not be anything owing on the land, don't you see?'

'You're kidding? You're saying this could've all been a scam?'

'Yes and it seems as though your solicitor is in on it too. I'm really sorry.'

Anger flashed across his eyes. 'I'm going to sort this out...'

Holly grabbed his arm, pulling him back from doing something he'd later regret.

'Don't be silly, you can't just charge right out of here. Dad said he's informed the local police, so let's just chill for a minute, yeah?'

Ben relented and slumped down on his sofa, head in hands.

'I can't bloody believe this.'

'Neither can I. So let's not do anything rash. We'll go to the light switch on and the charity ball and let the police handle it, yes?'

'Okay, but I'd better warn dad...'

'Best to wait, just incase he let slips he knows.'

'Alright, I'll wait, and I'm only doing this because of you,' he gazed into her eyes. 'Otherwise, I'd rip their heads...'

'No, you wouldn't... now come on, unless you're still leaving us and got nothing else to do, Betty needs a hand setting up her stall.'

Ben painted a smile on his face, his hardened expression relaxing.

'You drive a hard bargain, Holy Green. Come on then,' he got up. 'Let's go.'

The smell of ginger, cinnamon and hot chocolate permeated the air as they made their way onto the High Street.

'Smells like Christmas,' said Holly, gazing at the stalls as she passed.

'Smells like a rat,' Ben quipped looking in the direction of a man standing on the pavement, talking on the phone.

'Don't be hasty. I'll call dad soon as we're in Betty's, alright?'

'How can people live with themselves after destroying someone's life, huh?'

'I don't know, but you need to stop looking or you're going to antagonise him.'

Holly grabbed his arm, almost dragging him into the Betty's like a stroppy teenager.

'Oh look at you two, don't you make a lovely couple,' said Betty.

Ben nervously laughed and Holly felt her cheeks flush with embarrassment.

'We're just here to help. You do need help, don't you?'

'Of course we do, the more the merrier.'

'Good, because I brought help,' she nodded to Ben taking a seat on the stool. 'He was about to leave us, good job I caught him in time, right?' she loosened her scarf noting Betty's questionable expression.

'Yes, its good job you did. He's such a catch, isn't he?'

Holly cleared her throat. 'Alright, Bet, how about a latte, and what do you want?' she asked Ben who was checking his mobile.

'I'll have a regular coffee, thanks,' he replied, still focused on his phone.

'So, Bet, I've got some news from my dad,' she leaned on the bar, whispering.

'Oh?' she came closer.

Holly had a quick glance around the café. 'Well apparently all this selling of the farm is illegal. Ben's dad doesn't actually owe a penny. But shush, keep it to yourself for a while.'

Betty stood with her mouth gaped open.

The jingle on the door went and Holly swivelled around on her seat to see Susan and Clive walk into the café.

'Susan,' Betty called over. 'You'll want to hear this.'

Holly gave Betty a glare. 'Not yet,' she whispered. 'So have you arranged the meeting?' she asked in a normal tone of voice.

'Yes, we'll meet later this evening, perhaps Ben could fetch you?'

Ben looked up from his phone. 'Fetch who, what and where?'

Betty caught Holly's eye. 'I'd take that phone off him if I were you.'

'Betty asked if you could pick me up later for the meeting.'

'Of course I can. Not a problem. So, where do you want this stall?' he asked.

A KNOCK CAME AT THE cabin door. Holly finished buttoning up her coat and opened the door.

'You're looking dashing, are you ready?' asked Ben standing in a black double breasted coat and grey scarf. Holly's breath caught in her throat, struck by his beauty. No matter how much she hated herself for it, she couldn't deny he was a good-looking guy.

'Thank you, so do you,' she replied feeling like an idiot. Why did she say that?

Ben smiled; his grey eyes crinkling at the sides. 'Let me get my bag.' As she picked up her bag off the bed her phone rang. 'Excuse me a moment,' she said, stepping out and closing the door. 'Hi Dad, have you got any news?' she asked, walking to Ben's car. He opened the door for her and tucked in her coat before he closed it.

'I've had confirmation that an ex-employee of the solicitor has said he's done something similar before. We just have to prove it now.'

'So there's likely to be papers at his office?' asked Holly, hardly believing what she was thinking of doing.

'Maybe, Holly. Look, I'll have to call you back, okay?'

'Sure, dad and thanks.'

She put away her phone and turned to Ben.

'Dad said the lawyer has done this before. It's just a case of getting proof that he's been fiddling.'

'I can't believe he'd do that; the guy has been here longer than I have. He's a well-respected and trusted member of the community.'

'You asked if I was going to uncover something dark, looks like I did. Sorry.'

'Now what do we do?'

'Who is the secretary at the firm?'

'Mr Sandleson's wife, Linda. Why?'

'Does she have keys?'

'Holly – you can't do what I think you're going to do.'

'Why not? It's not exactly breaking and entering if you have keys.'

'I can't believe I'm actually considering this.'

'So are you going to be my partner in crime?'

'Holly, I've got to say, you've got guts girl. I'm in.'

Chapter Fifteen

It was early morning. Holly walked up and down the ice-slicked pavement outside the Gingerbread Cabin's gates, hoping Ben managed to convince Mrs Sandleson to let them into the office. She checked her mobile for the time when a car pulled up beside her. Mrs Sandleson, a petite lady waved at her with a cheery red lipstick smile from the passenger seat.

Holly got into the back. 'So glad you could make it, Mrs Sandleson.'

Mrs Sandleson held out a hand. 'Call me Linda, love and it's good to meet you.'

'Morning, Holly,' said Ben winking at her in the mirror. 'Linda is more than happy to help, aren't you?'

'Sure am. My goodness I feel like Angela Lansbury right now.'

Ben and Holly laughed.

'So the office is not open on the weekends then?' asked Holly, making sure no one would "accidently" turn up.

'No, I spoke with Harry yesterday after work. He mentioned something about an important meeting. Oh, you don't think it has anything to do with the farm business, do you?'

'More than likely,' replied Ben, tapping the steering wheel in frustration. 'I'm going to take the back road into town because the main road has been blocked off. Mrs Sandleson...'

'Linda, please...'

'Okay, Linda and you, Holly, go in through the back entrance of the shop and I'll wait outside incase anyone should show up.'

'Do you know what you might be looking for?' Holly asked Linda.

'I know he keeps all the files he doesn't want me to see kept locked in his desk drawer. I may be sixty-five but I'm not stupid like he must think I am.'

Ben and Holly laughed.

'Okay, guys, we're here.'

From the car they could see the main road that was busy with people setting up their stalls.

Holly got out of the car and followed Linda to the back door. 'We need to be in and out as quick as we can, do you know where he keeps the key for the desk drawer?'

'It's a combination code, love and it's his wife's birthday,' she winked, slipping the key through the lock.

They walked into the small storeroom that was full of boxes piled high with files and went through another door into the main office. Linda quickly drew the blinds on the front window that looked directly onto the main street and then pointed to a door at the side of the room.

'I won't be two shakes, wait there.' She whispered.

Holly stood anxiously in the office; her heart was pounding, and her nerves were shot. 'Do hurry, Linda,' she leaned back so she could see into the office.

'Nearly there,' she replied.

There were sounds of people passing outside, and someone had switched on the loudspeakers that were now blasting out Christmas music. Holly went to check on Linda when she heard rattling at the door. She turned sharply, zooming in on the door handle that was twisting.

'Shit, Linda, we'd better go,' she whispered, frantically pointing towards the door. 'Someone is trying to get in.'

Linda quickly sifted through piles of paper, yanked one out and put the rest back in the drawer.

'Got it, is the coast clear?'

Holly crept back into the room. Whoever was trying the door handle had now stopped.

'Yeah, come on, quickly.'

They both darted across the room to the back door and saw Harry striding towards them.

Holly's heart leapt to her throat. Linda tugged at her arm, pulling her under the desk set against a wall.

The door opened and Harry went into his office, leaving the front door open behind him. Holly felt Linda poke her on the back. She turned towards her.

'What?' she mouthed.

Linda pointed towards the back door.

Taking it as a sign to move she crawled out to the back room, got to her feet and then dashed across the garden to the gate crashing into Ben.

'Jeez, I'm sorry,' she said, straightening herself. She turned back and saw Linda closing the back gate behind her. 'It's Harry, he's in the office.' She gasped for breath.

'Let's get out of here,' said Ben running towards his car.

Once they were all in the car, they breathed heavily with relief.

'I honestly thought he'd see us,' said Holly.

'I saw him turn up and I panicked,' said Ben. 'Thank god you got out of there.'

Linda waved the papers about. 'I bloody well hope he's not looking for these, but then again, he has no reason to suspect us. The silly bugger hasn't even got a security camera.'

They all laughed, breaking the tension.

'I think this calls for a drink, don't you, Linda?' said Ben.

'Why not? I'll have a cheeky one before the Winterfest.'

WHILST BEN TOOK THE papers to the local sheriff, Linda and Holly caught up with Betty at her stall.

'How did it go?' she asked, handing over change to a customer.

'Really well, but I'll tell you everything later on.'

'Alright, love. The parade is about to start so why don't you get yourself a good spot and we'll talk at the café later.'

'Good idea, see you soon.' Holly turned to Linda. 'Are you coming?'

'Why not love,' she linked her arm. 'I haven't had this much fun in a long time.'

The crowd began cheering as a marching band playing Rudolph the Red Nosed Reindeer led the procession of floats. Holly rested her arms on the barrier, a little anxious whether Ben had managed to sort everything out with the police.

Linda patted her arm. 'Don't worry,' she shouted over the noise. 'The hard part is done.'

Holly nodded. 'Yeah, you're right, what can go wrong now?'

A float passed by with the local children dressed as elves. Holly began snapping pictures to include in her article. Slowly, she lowered the camera, hardly believing her eyes. A man who she immediately recognised as the imposter at the hotel came barging out of the crowd and onto the road. He pointed at Holly.

'I think I spoke too soon.'

The kids screamed and one by one the band stopped playing their instruments. The crowd roared with anger and confusion.

Holly felt her heart leap to her throat as the man skirted around the children towards her.

'Oh god, Linda, I'd better go.'

She pushed her way through the crowd and ran up the pavement trying to get her phone out of her pocket. About to reach the street corner, a horse and sleigh charged down the street and stopped right in front of her.

'Woah,' the man yelled.

Holly came to an abrupt stop by the kerb, staring at the man dressed as Father Christmas.

'Get on,' he thumbed to the back of the sleigh.

'Since when does Father Christmas have horses?' she wondered and then remembered she was being pursued.

Holly climbed onto the back of the sleigh to a round of applause from the audience. The sleigh took off down the road leaving her holding on for dear life.

'Jeez, Santa, don't you observe the speed limits,' she yelled, thinking it was Ben dressed up.

Police sirens now wailed in the distance. Holly scrambled to the seat, looked behind her and saw a police car pull up and arrest the man.

'Where are we going?' she asked but there was still no answer. She climbed over to the front seat and got a good look at the Santa.

'Do I know you?' she asked, grabbing hold of the seat. 'And where are you taking me?' she demanded as the sleigh pulled outside the gate to the Tree farm.

'Holly?' shouted Ben, running towards her.

Holly jumped off the sleigh, finding comfort in Ben's arms.

'The guy tried to grab me at the parade,' she panted, out of breath.

'It's okay, everything's okay now.' He smoothed her hair. 'The police have got him and arrested Walker. It's thanks to you that the farm is safe.'

'Oh I need to say thanks to...' she lifted her head from Ben's shoulder but the sleigh had gone.

'Where the hell did he go?'

'I don't know, but you made quite an entrance. Wait a minute, that sleigh wasn't the one in the parade, where did it come from?'

'What's this?' asked Holly, walking to the kerb.

A small red parcel with a gold bow on top was the only thing left on the road where the sleigh had parked.

Ben followed.

'It's for us.' She read the tag again. 'For Ben and Holly, take good care of it, love "FC,"'

'Who's FC?'

Holly shrugged and opened the wrapping. 'Oh wait, you don't think...nah, it can't be. I mean, he's not...'

'Real?'

Holly continued with the unwrapping and opened the lid of the box. Inside was a small tree.

'Ben,' she gasped and handed him the box.

'A tree? Wow. This is just like how the story goes. You don't think?'

Holly shook her head. 'Nah...there's no way that guy was...*him*. Come on, we're fully grown adults for crying out loud.'

'Maybe we should get back to the parade, yeah?' Ben suggested and took Holly's arm. 'And then later we can go for that dinner we arranged at the start of the week.'

Chapter Sixteen

She removed her glasses and switched off her laptop. To her relief, the article was done, well ahead of the deadline and it even had a happy ending, except she wasn't ready to send it to Walker just yet.

She took her coat off the back of the chair, grabbed her car keys from the pocket and picked up her suitcase off the bed. At least her car was fixed, and she could go home. Not that she was looking forward to it. The idea of going back to her apartment filled her with dread. While she got the rest of her things together, she thought about staying with her parents this Christmas Eve so she wouldn't be alone, surround by memories.

Taking another look outside the window, at the snow flurries still falling in the dull, grey afternoon, she knew she'd miss this place. Her thoughts shifted to Ben. Though he had agreed to stay on the farm with his uncle, it was with a heavy heart she was leaving. She trudged across the compound to Susie's cabin and rang the bell at the reception. Susie came out of her office.

'You're leaving us?' she stuck out her bottom lip.

'Unfortunately, yes,' Holly put down her luggage and opened her handbag. 'How much do

I owe you for the extra few days?' she asked, leafing through her credit cards.

'Are you kidding?'

Holly looked up, surprised.

'After what you did for us, it's on the house, isn't that right, Clive,' she shouted towards the door.

Holly turned around to see Clive coming in the door dragging a tree behind him.

'Absolutely and before I forget, Holly, I saw Ben just earlier, he sold me the tree.'

'Did he?' she felt her cheeks flush. 'Oh wait, let me give you a hand with that.' She took hold of the bottom half and helped carry it to the pot waiting by reception.

Susie also ran around the counter to help him.

'Need a hand?'

'It's okay, love. So are we going to see you back here?' Clive asked Holly.

'Of course, I'll be back. So did Ben say anything at all?' She asked as casually as she could, but Susie saw right through her.

'I still think you'd both make a great couple. Why don't you pop on over there before you go, you know, just to see if any sparks fly?'

Clive caught Holly's eyes. 'Ignore her. You just do what you feel is right.'

'Well, I'll see, so, it was nice to meet you both. Thank you for your hospitality. I'll try to squeeze in a few good words about the cabins for you.'

Susie pulled her in for a hug. 'It was nice having you and remember what I said about you and Ben,' she whispered.

Holly smiled and nodded. 'I will do.' She picked up her luggage and left the hotel, torn about what she should do for the best.

After spending the next evening at her local café going over her article, she finally hit send.

The next morning, she walked into her office to an excited bunch of work colleagues with their heads buried in pieces of A4 paper. She noticed their eyes drew upwards when she passed, which was followed by whispers, nudges and pointing in her direction.

'What's the matter with everyone?' she asked Emily as she dumped her bag on her desk. It was then she saw Emily had copies of whatever everyone else was reading.

'You're back,' she got up from her seat and flung her arms around her. 'So how was it, tell me more about Ben and the farm,' she swooned.

'Oh you're kidding me, right? Walker has issued everyone with a preview copy?'

'You know she does it every year, but I've got to be honest, Holly, this is the best story by far.'

Relieved, Holly sat down in her chair and took off her coat.

'You think?'

'Do I think? I *know*. It's full of mystery, intrigue, bad guys and a sexy guy.'

'Good god, you and sexy guys.' Holly rolled her eyes at her and switched on her PC.

'Do you have a picture of you together, I'd love to see what he looks like for real?'

'Um,' Holly pulled her phone out of her coat pocket. 'I'm not sure…'

'I bet you do. Hand it over, girl.'

Holly relented and flipped through her photos, finding one of her and Ben at the Winterfest.

'I think someone is in love.' Emily sang the words.

'What? No, gosh, Emily, I've only just lost Dan.'

'Holly, it has been over a year, and don't you think he'd be happy for you. *And*,' she looked at the picture. 'This Ben chap seems very nice, especially from the messages you sent me about him.'

'Yeah, well,' she took back her phone. 'He's got his life and I've got mine.'

'You don't mean that. Anyway, come for lunch with me later. I've missed my partner in crime,' she pouted.

Holly thought back to the incident at the solicitor's office and chuckled to herself. 'Why not, it's a date and besides there's something I've got to tell you that I couldn't put in the article.'

Strolling down busy Oxford Street, laden with shopping bags Emily pointed towards a coffee shop.

'I think we've shopped until we dropped, huh?' She slumped down on a chair.

Over a latte, Holly told her about Snowdonia and then remembered the gift her mother had given her from Dan.

'Did I tell you?'

'Tell me what?' she asked.

'When I went home, mum remembered she had something of Dan's to give me,' she reached into her jumper to show her the necklace, but she couldn't find it. 'Oh no, it's gone. My necklace is gone.' She frantically looked around the floor.

'What's missing?'

'The necklace Dan gave me.'

Emily joined in the search. 'Are you sure it isn't caught on your jumper?'

'I'm not taking my jumper off in here.'

'Well when did you last notice it?'

'On my way home from Snowdonia.'

'Well check the car later.'

'WELL THAT'S THAT, IT'S gone,' Holly exhaled deeply and passed Emily a glass of Prosecco.

'It can't have got far. Hey, maybe you should call the place you stayed in Snowdonia.'

Holly knew what she really meant. 'I'm not calling Ben if that's what you're insinuating.'

'Oh well,' she sipped her drink. 'It was just a suggestion.'

'Okay, I'll phone, but only because I've had bit of Dutch courage,' she raised her glass. She brought Ben's number on her screen and called. 'It's ringing, happy now?' she whispered.

The phone rang several times.

'Hello, Holly,' said a sprightly female voice.

'Hi, who am I speaking to?' she asked, thinking she rang the wrong number.

'It's Kirsty, from the diner. I served you a couple of times.'

'Oh, sorry, I thought I rang Ben's number,' she said, confused. She wasn't sure if she had the number of the café in her phone.

'It is his number. I'm sorry he can't come to the phone right now, he's in the bathroom.'

Shocked, and more upset than she thought she'd be, she was about to ask her if she could leave a message when the phone clicked on the other end.

'Well?' asked Emily.

'It looks like he's on a date or something.' She got up and went to the kitchen.

'Wait, what? Did he tell you that? What a nerve.' Emily slammed her glass on the counter. 'You should tell him he shouldn't have led you on.'

'Well, he didn't really. We went out to lunch, once. But...I thought he liked me.'

'Give me your phone. I'll text him.'

'No. I think this is a sign,' she said, filling another glass with wine.

'Oh don't talk to me about signs, it's all bull. The fact is that bitch has your man and you need to get him back.'

'Emily, he wasn't mine to begin with.'

'Oh really? He saved your butt when your car broke down. Jeez, Hols, you practically spent all week with him. Wait a minute, does that mean it's a... sign?' she winked.

'When you put it like that then maybe...'

'Go on, send him a message and ask him how he is. For all you know that girl maybe playing with you. Didn't you call them the she-devils,' Emily laughed.

'Okay, but maybe tomorrow...'

Chapter Seventeen

Christmas Eve

The 5 a.m. alarm sounded, waking Holly. She patted around her bed for her phone, picked it up and then held it close to her face. ARTICLE PRINTED

Now fully awake, she jumped out of bed, ran into the living room, and grabbed her coat draped over the back of the sofa. Overcome with excitement, she didn't have time to think about an outfit and so she pulled on her boots over her pyjama bottoms and left the house, hoping to catch the first batch of newspapers delivered to her local newsagents.

Milo's newsagents were at the end of her road, a place she'd frequent on her way to work. She'd normally buy a bar of chocolate and a bottle of water that almost always turned into a chat about how much she hated her job. Power walking to the shop, which she could see had its lights' on, she began to run the rest of the way.

'Slow down, Miss Green,' said a shocked Milo stacking newspapers on the counter.

She pointed to The World newspaper while she tried to get her breath back.

'By the way you've come blazing in here, you'd think you have an article in there?' he chuckled, getting to his feet.

Holly nodded enthusiastically.

'I do, Milo, about bloody time eh.'

'What is it?' he asked, picking up a copy and flipping through it.

'It's only *the* most anticipated, most loved Christmas feature of the season.'

'Well blow me down. Don't tell me they actually saw you're worth and gave you a shot?'

Milo passed her the paper.

'That they did, Milo,' she replied staring at her two-page spread. 'That they did.'

'One Christmas in Snowdonia.'

Stepping out of Milo's newsagents she anxiously flipped through the special Christmas edition of The World. Fresh off the press, the smell of ink was still apparent on the thick offering that also included a glossy television guide inside.

The sun hadn't risen; and the cold December morning had her pacing around glare of the shops' light to keep some semblance of warmth.

'I wish you could see this Dan,' she mumbled, her breath fanning out like puffs of cloud.

Thinking it was best to get back to the flat, she walked along the quiet, frosted pavement as curtains swished open, and lights flickered on in the Victorian terraces. She berated herself for thinking of the past. Today wasn't a day to feel bad, today meant to be a celebration. She began to count her footsteps to distract her from thoughts and feelings she wished had stayed buried, but the report along with the anniversary of Daniels's passing just made it so difficult. She turned the corner onto the High Street. Council workers in luminous jackets were busy fixing the Christmas lights. *Fixing Christmas lights*, she wondered, at this hour? She hoped to slip by, unnoticed and preferably unrecognized, but a man who had been whistling paused when she passed.

'Good morning,' he waved at her from the crane. 'Awfully cold, isn't it?' he shouts, dangling a string of coloured lights.

'Morning,' she replied, waving the paper. 'It's bloody freezing.' The locals were a friendly bunch. Everyone knew everyone and their business in Hilltop.

'Ah, miss Green. I just picked up the paper. I loved your article.'

'Thank you, you've made my day.'

As she put her family's Christmas presents into a bag on her bed, her foot hit something underneath. Curious to see what it was, she lifted her bedspread to find a cardboard box with Dan's name on it her mother had packed away for her. She thought for a moment, trying to remember what was in there but she couldn't think. She dropped the bedspread, but a niggling feeling to look at the contents, to feel close to him again prompted her to bend down and pull out the box.

'What do we have here,' she muttered, opening the lid. Inside there were piles of papers and photographs. She tipped the contents over her fleece blanket and sat down, sifting through it. She smiled at pictures of him with his friends at the barracks, remembering all the stories he used to tell her. Looking at the picture of all his workmates, she was about to put it down when a familiar face in the background caught her eye. She looked closely, threw the picture down and then picked it back up again.

'It can't be,' she shrieked. 'Ben?' Her heart began to race. She got up, shaking with excitement and began pacing the room as thoughts swirled around her head.

'Oh my god, oh my god, oh my god...what are the bloody chances.'

She snatched her phone from the bed and thought about calling Ben, but her hands couldn't stop shaking to scroll for the number. About to head out of her room to get a drink from the kitchen, her front door knocked.

'I'm coming, hang on,' she shouted, rushing through the living room. She yanked open the front door to an excited Emily.

'Here I am,' cried Emily, bounding into the house waving the newspaper. 'Do you realise you're famous, Miss Green. Everyone is raving about this story. And your picture, well what can I say...'

Holly could see Emily was waiting for a response from her, but all that came out of her mouth was gibberish. Emily then noticed something wasn't right.

'Holly...you're scaring me.'

Holly held out the photograph.

'Look at this, who do you see.'

Emily frowned. 'What?' She took the picture and gave it a quick scan. 'I see Dan when he was in the army.'

'Yes, it's Dan's regiment, but apart from Dan, you may see someone else you'll recognise.'

Emily looked again. 'Wait a minute...he looks like...but it can't be the guy from the paper today. It's not possible.'

'It's Ben. He was in the same regiment as Dan, and I didn't know.'

'You didn't know he was in the army?'

'He told me but we didn't really discuss it.'

'Well hell's spells,' Emily flounced down on the sofa. 'Holly, you need call Ben right this minute. Do you realise what this is. It's fate, that's what it is.'

'I tried to call, but what if miss prissy pants answers again.'

Emily got back up. 'If you don't call him, I will.'

'Okay, okay, chill out, girl.'

She dialled his number, but it kept ringing.

'Leave a message,' Emily whispered.

'Hi Ben, it's Holly. If you get this message, could you please call me back? Thanks.' She exhaled and went to her drink cabinet. 'I know it's early...'

'No, no, no, you're dropping me off at my parent's later and I need you sober. I'll make us a coffee until your head has stopped spinning with all this excitement,' she chuckled.

'Yeah, good point. I'll make up for it later.'

'So what are you going to say to him?' she asked, filling up the kettle.

'What can I say,' she leaned against the counter. 'I spent a week with a man who knew my fiancé. How is that even possible?'

'It's like a little Christmas miracle, eh.'

'Sure is, hey after this, we should get going. My parents are taking me out to lunch tonight to celebrate the article, but I don't know if I'm up to it now.'

'Course you are and you'll let me know when he calls, huh? I want to know everything.'

Holly pulled up outside Emily's family home, a red bricked terrace in the suburbs covered with Christmas lights. 'Have a nice Christmas,' she waved.

'I want to know everything,' shouted Emily standing on the pavement.

Before Holly pulled off, she checked her phone but there was no reply from Ben. The worry was gnawing away inside her, so she dialled Susie instead.

'Hello, Susie...'

'Holly. What a nice surprise. Oh and before I forget, Merry Christmas and many congratulations on the article. It was wonderful, everyone is talking about it.'

'That's great to hear, Susie. The reason I'm calling is, I've been trying to get a hold of Ben for a while...'

'You have?'

'Yeah, is he still around?'

'Of course he is. For some reason he turned down the job and is now back working with his dad. He's been a bit miserable mind you since you've gone. Oh I don't know if I should've told you that... Oh well, but I know the poor bugger lost his phone the day after you went home.'

'He did? Then why did Kirsty from the café answer it?'

'Kirsty did what? Betty sacked her the other day, love so I don't know. Maybe you should call Betty and ask her.'

'Okay, thanks Susie. Have a lovely Christmas.'

'Come and visit us sometime, don't be a stranger.'

'I'll be back soon, see you, Susie.'

Damn, she thought. It was all confusing. If he thought about her, why hasn't he made an effort to call? Then again, he did lose his phone, or did he? Even so, why would Kirsty answer it?

'Shut up Holly, just stop thinking the worst and drive.' She pulled out, deciding to call Betty when she got to her parents.

When she arrived at her parents, her dad was out on the front lawn testing out his snow machine.

Holly coughed to get his attention.

'Holly, come here and give your old dad a hug,' he said with outstretched arms. 'I'm very proud of you, the story was lovely.'

'Thanks Dad. Mum inside?'

'Yeah, she's either in the kitchen or packing last minute presents. She doesn't half go overboard.'

'It's once a year, dad what are you complaining about?'

'Oh someone has changed their tune, I see.'

The house smelled of freshly baked cakes and apple and cinnamon candles that were burning on the radiator cover when she entered. She took off her coat and hung it on the balustrade.

'Mum, it's me,' she yelled, making her way to the kitchen.

Delina almost crashed into her at the door. 'Bloody heck, you gave me a fright.' She pulled her in for a hug and went back to her oven where she was stirring a pot of mulled wine.

Holly pulled out a chair at the table and sat down. 'You'll never guess what?'

Delina turned sharply. 'What? Oh I read the article, it was fantastic. Look, I even bought a frame to put it in,' she pointed the wooden spoon to the worktop.

'Why am I not surprised? Anyway, mum, something horrible has happened. I lost the locket somewhere in Snowdonia.'

'You're joking? Have you called the place you stayed at?'

'I did, and oh, that reminds me, I meant to call the café, too. Give me a minute, mum.' She went out the back garden, closing the door behind her. The neighbour's cat jumped off the fence and began rubbing its side against her legs.

The phone rang and rang. Thinking they were busy too answer, as she was about to end the call, she heard Betty's cheery voice on the other end.

'Hello, Betty, it's me, Holly.'

'Hello, love, I didn't expect to hear from you so soon. Missing us, are you?'

Holly laughed. 'Of course. I do have a reason for calling. I'm looking Ben. I've tried calling him on his phone, but it keeps ringing. The last time Kirsty answered...'

'Kirsty? Do you mean the girl who worked here?'

'Yes.'

'I've sacked her. Apparently Ben lost his phone here and she didn't turn it in the day she found it. It must've been when you answered. Oh the conniving, lying...'

'Oh, so why hasn't he been answering me then? I hope I haven't done anything to offend him.'

'I couldn't tell you, I heard from Harry that he said he had to go somewhere and mightn't be back for a little while.'

'Okay, Betty, thanks, and Merry Christmas. Pass it on to everyone from me, will you?'

'Of course I will. I hope he gets in touch; you were so good together, you know.'

About to end the call, Holly remembered her locket. 'Oh, there was one other thing. I lost a heart shaped locket while I was there. Has anyone found it?'

'One minute.'

Holly could hear Betty shouting in the background.

'No, I'm sorry, nobody has found anything. If I do hear anything, I'll call you.'

'Thanks, Betty, have a nice Christmas.'

'You too. Come back and visit us soon, won't you?'

'I will, bye.'

Holly bent down to pet the cat and then went back into the kitchen.

'Any luck,' asked mum.

Holly shook her head. 'Nah. Is the mulled wine ready, if so can I have some?' she asked, trying to mask her disappointment.

'Of course. And try not to worry, it'll turn up so try not to dwell on it.'

'I hope so.' Her thoughts went to Ben. She thanked her mother for the wine and went into the living room; the regret of not telling him how she truly felt eating away at her.

Her brother was sat on the sofa eating pizza. 'Alright, Holly, I've got your favourite film on here, Santa Claus the Movie.' He pointed at the screen.

Holly slumped down on the sofa, next to the Christmas tree that was brimming with presents.

'Just like when we were kids, eh, Scott.'

'I still am a kid, thank you very much,' he laughed, offering her a slice of pizza from a box. 'Oh and congrats on the article, it was a damn good read, and you know I'm not joking because reading and me don't mix.'

'Don't I know it,' she reached out to grab a slice.

Her father came into the room. 'Come on, you pair of lazy bones, I'm treating us all to a drink at the pub.'

Holly groaned.

'Dad, I'm quite comfortable here.'

Scott passed Holly the pizza. 'Here you go, sis. I'm not passing up free alcohol. Come on, dad.'

'I think that's the quickest the boy has moved.'

'Don't forget the time when you took him to buy a Sega Mega drive,' Holly laughed.

'So aren't you coming?'

'Nah, I'm happy here for a bit.'

'Well you know where we are if you change your mind.'

'Alright, dad.'

Once her brother and father had left, she made herself comfortable on the sofa and checked her phone. There were many messages of congratulations but the person she wanted to hear from the most was unreachable. She pulled the blanket off the back of the sofa and rested her head on the cushion.

'Holly, answer your phone, will you?' Delina shouted.

Holly opened her eyes, not remembering falling asleep and patted around the sofa for her phone. She picked it up, trying to focus on the caller ID.

'Ben.' She pressed the accept button. 'Is that you this time?' she asked.

'It's me, Holly. Look, I'm sorry for what happened. Kirsty got hold of my phone...'

'It's okay, I found out from Betty. How are you?'

'I'm good now I hear your voice. I was wondering...'

'What?'

'How you would you feel about having a visitor tonight. I know it's Christmas Eve and everything...'

'A visitor?' she then smiled. 'Well Santa is coming...'

'Funny, but I was talking about me. I'm on my way to London, so if I could have your address, please.'

'You're coming to see me? Now...'

'You sound terrified,' he laughed.

'No, I'm not; really...it'll be so good to see you.' She replied, trying to wrap her head around the whole situation. She then remembered the photograph and the many questions she wanted to ask. Perhaps he had figured out who she was too?

'That's nice to hear, because I missed you and...I'll tell you what, give me your address and I'll see you in a short while. Then we can talk, alright?'

'I'm at my parents, so, it's 39 Elmsgrove Avenue, Whittlegreen.'

'Thanks, and I'll see you soon.'

She put the phone down in shock.

'Mum, you need to hear this.'

Delina came rushing into the living room.

'What's wrong?'

'I've got a visitor coming this evening, he's...'

'He?'

'Don't get excited, he's just a friend. His name is Ben. I met him in Snowdonia.'

'That's the guy who was mentioned in your article?'

Holly nodded and got up off the sofa. 'Yes, that's him. I don't know what he wants, but don't go making mountains out of molehills, please. Now, I'm just going to my room for a minute.'

'Holly, wait a second,' said Delina following her into the hallway. 'I hope this works out for you, you know what I mean.' She gave her an affectionate rub on her arm.

'You just can't help yourself, can you? Thanks mum. I hope Dan would approve.'

'I bet he orchestrated the whole thing,' she smiled and went into the kitchen.

Holly raced up the stairs to her room, hoping in some small way it was true. She looked at herself in her mirror and decided she needed to change her clothes. The whole situation seemed surreal.

Twenty minutes later, as she was about to head downstairs, she heard the sound of a car pulling up outside. She put down her hairbrush and pulled back the blinds. Her stomach flipped when she saw Ben's car parked on the opposite side of the road. Just as she was about to drop the blind and get to the door before her mother had the chance, she saw Mrs Turnbull yank open her front door.

'You can't park there, it's for private parking only, now move it.' She waved her walking stick.

'I'm really sorry,' replied Ben standing in the middle of the road. 'There's nowhere else to park.'

Holly burst out laughing.

'You've got five minutes, you bloody punk, or I'll call the police.'

Ben pushed back his hair and looked over at Holly's house and then back at Mrs Turnbull.

'I promise I won't be five minutes,' he held up his hands as though he was being interrogated. He ran up the garden path, pressed the doorbell several times and just as she was about to dash downstairs to answer it, she heard her mother shout out that she had got it.

'Hi, is this Holly's house?'

'You must be Ben?'

'Yes, that's right.'

'Come in, come in, I'll get her for you.'

Holly stood on top of the stairs; she met Ben's eyes and ran down to greet him. 'It's great to see you.'

'You too,' he pulled her in for a hug.

'Mum, this Ben, the one I was telling you about.'

'Nice to meet you, Mrs Green,' he shook her hand.

'Likewise, and you can call me Delina. I can't tell you how nice it is to see a smile on my girl's face.' She gave Holly a little nudge. 'Would you like a cup of tea or something stronger?' she asked.

Holly glared at her, willing her out the kitchen.

'Mum, give him a minute,' she took his arm, guiding him into the living room, hoping her mother had got the hint. She felt like a teenager all over again. 'Take a seat,' she gestured to the sofa, and then realised it was full of empty pizza boxes, a blanket and a box of tissues.

It looked as though someone was having a pathetic pity party. How embarrassing, she thought. 'Ignore all this, it's my brother's.' She picked up her things and shoved them to the other side of the sofa.

'Well he looks like he knows how to throw a good party. Shame I wasn't invited.'

'If you were here half hour ago, you'd have been most welcomed. He's now at the pub with my dad. So...' she sat on the chair next to him and cleared her throat.

Ben took her hand.

'Could we go for a drive? There's something I really must talk to you about.'

'Are you sure it's not because Mrs Turnbull threatened you with the police?' She then laughed.

'That too. She was terrifying,' he mocked her waving her stick.

'She's really harmless, so you can leave the car there if you want. We could go for a walk.'

'That sounds even better. It's not like its alien to us. You know; the walk around the farm...'

'Of course, it was a lovely walk. Um,' she pointed to the door. 'I'll just let mum know we'll have tea later.'

As she got up, Delina came into the room with a tray of tea and freshly baked cookies. She set it down on the table.

'Mum, we're just going to pop out for a minute, we won't be long.'

'Sorry, Mrs Green, I promise I won't keep her long. I just have some things I need to talk to her about.'

'Of course. It was lovely to meet you, and I'm so glad your farm has been saved. It was such a wonderful story.'

'Oh thank you, yes, my father is happy too. We owe Holly a lot.'

Ben took Holly's hand as they walked to the door. With her other hand, she grabbed her coat from the balustrade and waved to her mother standing in the living room with the biggest smile she'd seen for a while.

'There's a park just down the road with a little pond. I used to play there when I was a kid. I haven't been in years, so it'll be a nice to see what they've done with the place.'

'Sure, whatever you want. This is a nice little area.' He mused, looking around.

'It's okay, I guess. Worse places to grow up than this, I suppose,' she shrugged, wishing he would get to the point of him being here.

Ben pushed open the gate that led them onto a winding concrete path. Trees bordered the way to the pond and to an empty bench.

'It's like that night you found me after you escaped from the meeting,' Ben chuckled.

'Yeah, except this is no Snowdonia.'

'Snowdonia or not, I'm happy because you're here.' He squeezed her hand.

Ben gestured her to the bench, sat down and then twisted to face her. 'Holly, I have something to give you.' He reached into his jacket pocket and then took her hand. 'Open your hand.'

Holly unfolded her hand and looked down. Shining back at her was her gold locket. She took a sharp intake of breath.

'It's my locket, where did you find it?'

'I found it by the Christmas tree. Holly, there's something else I've got to tell you.'

'No, wait.' Tears stained her eyes. 'There's something I need to ask you first...you were in the same regiment as my Dan, weren't you? You knew Dan Locke?'

'I did and it wasn't until I found your locket that I knew who you were...'

'How do you mean. It just says Dan. There are millions of Dan's in the world.'

'He bought it the day before we were shipped out. I remember him showing it to all the boys when he got back. He was so excited about giving it to you, and he was going to, but it was another guy who suggested he'd give it to your mother to give you on Christmas Day.'

'Oh my goodness, so I'd have something to open from him on the day.' Her lips quivered.

Ben took her hand.

'I'm so happy I've met you. In some small way I feel like I already know you better than I originally thought.'

Holly looked at him through her tear-stained eyes.

'I mean, he used to talk about you all the time. He was a good bloke and he loved you very much. I just hope I'm not treading on toes by being here.'

Holly shook her head. 'He did love me very much and it's lovely to hear from someone who shared his profession,' her voice broke.

'Am I upsetting you? Do you want me to shut up or leave?'

She squeezed his hand. 'No, I don't want you to go anywhere. Do you believe in miracles, Ben? Because right now, I truly believe he brought us together and if you're not planning on driving back to Snowdonia tonight, you're more than welcome to celebrate Christmas with us.'

'I'd really love that, thank you, and if you're not too busy, maybe you'd accompany me back to Christmas Village tomorrow? You still owe me a date at the Lodge.'

'So it's a date now is it?'

Ben nodded.

'I think we're at that point in our relatively short, but awesome relationship to call it a date, yes. If that's what you want? No pressure at all.'

'I'd love that very much, but just one question. Did you manage to find out who the Father Christmas was that saved me?'

'Heck, I forgot to tell you. You're not going to believe this, but the sleigh was found by the Christmas tree. No Father Christmas and no horse, except for a few boot footprints in the snow leading to the tree.

My father has his suspicions, but…Father Christmas isn't real? Or is he?' He said in all seriousness.

'I think that's another story, Ben,' Holly laughed. She stood up and held out her hand. 'Come on, it's Christmas Eve and my parents will be thinking I've deserted Christmas again.'

www.ingramcontent.com/pod-product-compliance
Lightning Source LLC
Chambersburg PA
CBHW031740150726
47989CB00006B/2539